LITTLE GIRL LOST

CRIMSON FALLS NOVELLA

LAURÈN LEE

LITTLE GIRL LOST

For Emerald O'Brien for organizing the Crimson Falls series and being a great friend!

CRIMSON FALLS

The worst place to be in early October is the town of Crimson Falls.

In the late 1800's, two brothers stumbled upon an unnamed village, surrounded by thick forest and fresh water to keep them protected and alive. The brothers were cruel men who wanted a home to call their own. In their darkest hour, the brothers slaughtered the villagers, dumping their bodies over the waterfall at the edge of town. People say the water ran red for weeks, giving the town its terrible name.

Ever since that horrible anniversary, Crimson Falls is haunted by its past with a present filled with violence and danger. Every October is filled with fear...and for good reason. On October 13th, the dreaded Founders Day, all the town's crime comes to a head. And by the 14th, fewer will be alive than before.

Crimson Falls is a fictional town, created and shared by 8 mystery, suspense, and thriller authors. Each novella paints a picture about life in Crimson Falls and the insanity that takes place leading up to Founders Day. Do you dare to read them all?

2019

CHAPTER ONE

SUNDAY, OCTOBER 6, 2019

"Harper? Did you leave yet?" a woman's raspy voice called from within the two-story, decade-old Victorian house.

"Not yet, Mama. Putting my coat on now!" a young girl of tiny stature zipped up her hot pink jacket with a fleece-lined hood. She reached for her pack of Bubbilicious gum on her nightstand, unwrapped a piece of the watermelon treat, and put the wrapper in her pocket.

The redheaded girl with locks reaching her backside looked out the window. In the distance, a dreadful storm cloud headed her way. She hoped more than anything the storm would veer off and miss them, but it tended to rain more often than not this time of the year. Harper planned to visit her friend Lillian at her house. It was a couple of miles away, but Harper could ride her shiny new plum bike nearly anywhere in town.

Harper's parents, both lawyers, weren't always so approving of their daughter's ventures around Crimson Falls. After all, Harper had only just turned ten. But her parents worked long hours and couldn't always drive her to activities outside of their neighborhood. After many arguments and near begging on Harper's part, her parents agreed she could ride her bike to friends' houses as long as the parents would be home and she was back before the streetlights turned on.

Naturally, as the daughter of lawyers, Harper pled her case that a set time for coming home would be more prudent as the street lights came on earlier and earlier in the fall. It would severely cut into her playing time and by December, she wouldn't have enough time to play at all.

Her parents, though, wouldn't concede on that point and reinforced the new rule. One strike against the girl would cause her to lose her newly acquired privilege temporarily. Harper's parents loved her very much but also set high standards and rules for their daughter.

Sandy Golden, with a basket of dirty clothes on her hip and a leather-bound briefcase in her other hand, strode into the kitchen, pink-faced, and her strawberry-blonde hair up in a messy bun. She was a trusts and estates lawyer in town and business boomed for her regularly. Crimson Falls residents dealt with a slew of deaths, especially in October, which not only kept the population down but led to the need for wills and estates to be settled.

Sandy's husband, Kyle, practiced in many different aspects of law at the same firm. Sandy and Kyle founded Golden & Golden soon after they married almost fifteen years previously. They didn't want to work for Bud Jakobs, the oldest lawyer in town, so they started their firm. About half of Crimson Falls went to Bud and the other half when to Golden & Golden.

"Put on some gloves, Harper. It's chilly outside. And why are you wearing your new pink sneakers? They're going to get all muddy playing outside!"

Harper wrinkled her nose and rolled her eyes. "I'll be careful, Mom. Sheesh. I'm just going to Lillian's house."

Sandy carefully eyed her stubborn daughter. She was about to protest but the buzzer went off in the laundry room, and her hip ached with the basket of the past week's clothes digging into her side.

"All right. Well, you know the rule—"

"Be home before the streetlights come on," Harper chirped. "I know. I know."

Harper reached for the backdoor and in the last moment before she stepped outside into the frigid autumn air, she turned around and smiled at her mother. Little did she know, it would be the last time she'd ever see her again.

————

HARPER PUT on her silver holographic helmet and mounted her bike. Silver and white glittery streamers poked out from the handlebars on either side and a silver horn lay in the middle of them, too. She sped up her street and past the neighboring houses older than even her grandparents' parents.

Crimson Falls, a small town at least a half hour from any neighboring city, only lay home to about one thousand people. Harper didn't mind living in a small town, but it made it damn near impossible to do anything without it getting back to her parents. She couldn't even jaywalk without someone mentioning it to her mother. Everyone knew each other's business and made it a point to stir the pot when necessary. And yet, they all had each other's backs. It was a small community, but a tough-as-nails one, too. When you hurt one, you hurt them all.

Harper pedaled her heart out despite the frosty chill in the air. She couldn't wait to go to Lillian's house and play with her new Barbie mansion. Her friend boasted about it at school, and now Harper'd have the chance to see if it was all it was cracked up to be.

Harper sped down Lillian's street with a rumbling stomach and a desire to enjoy the last day of the weekend. Harper loved school and learning, especially English, but weekends were always so much better. Not only did she see her parents more on Saturday and Sunday, but she had more time to spend with her friends, too.

She turned into Lillian's concrete driveway and hopped off her bicycle. Harper leaned it against the garage and sprinted into Lillian's house. Her friend screeched at her arrival, and they jumped up and down and hugged each other jovially.

For the next handful of hours, the girls played with Lillian's Barbies, feasted on Twinkies and Pizza Bites, and gossiped about the girls and boys at their school. Harper's parents didn't allow her to consume any junk food, so she took full advantage of the perks at Lillian's house.

Lillian's parents sat at the kitchen table and poured over stacks of papers, a calculator and a pen in each hand. Lillian's mother frowned while her father huffed and puffed. Harper and Lillian knew better than to disturb them, so they played in Lillian's bedroom.

"What are you going to ask for for Christmas?" Lillian questioned her best friend.

"I don't know," Harper replied as she stuck her tongue out in concentration. She attempted to pull a princess dress onto her Barbie, but it didn't quite fit.

"Maybe you could get a Barbie Mansion just like me?" Lillian suggested.

"Yeah, I don't know. Maybe," Harper replied. "I kind of want this jewelry-making kit I saw on the TV."

"Ooohh cool! If you get it, can I come over and make a necklace?"

Harper finally pulled the dress onto her Barbie and pranced her around, pretending the doll was speaking instead of her.

"Girls? Ready for dinner?" Lillian's mother called to them.

Harper jumped at the sound of Mrs. Chase's voice and glanced outside. The sun danced toward the horizon as it set on Crimson Falls. The street lamps would be on soon. Harper's heart pounded in her chest and images of losing her bike, and the ability to come to play with Lillian, sped into her consciousness.

"I have to go!" she fretted.

"Aw, man, really? You're going to miss Sloppy Joe night," Lillian countered.

Harper threw her arms around her friend and handed her the Barbie she'd borrowed for the afternoon.

"See you at school!" Harper raced down the stairs and out of the house before Lillian could reply.

Outside, the dark cloud from earlier hovered over the city, completely blocking out any traces of the sun she'd witnessed only minutes ago. Leaves twirled in the streets and tore away from the branches high in the sky. Off in the distance, one street lamp flickered on, and more followed suit like a stack of dominoes.

"No!" Harper cried. She would be late and surely disciplined for it.

She pedaled as though her life depended on it. Harper raced through the desolate streets of Crimson Falls. On Sunday nights, most people were inside having dinner with their families. On any night in October, most people avoided venturing outside at all if they could avoid it. Harper attributed her parents' permission to go to Lillian's house at all to the fact they probably hadn't realized it was October already.

By now, sweat trickled down Harper's petite back, and all the street lamps around her were ignited. She was late and in so, so much trouble. Still, she pedaled hard and pretended to be a Nascar car racer, destined to come in first and hold up the golden trophy above her head.

Ahead, parallel to a playground, the sidewalk turned unpredictable and cracked. Harper knew the area well and planned to ride in the street for the next block to avoid the uneven concrete. However, before she had the chance to steer away, she hit a bump in the sidewalk and launched off her bike. She landed on her stomach, only catching herself with her bare hands. She'd left her gloves at Lillian's, and her palms ached as blood dripped from the scrapes. Tears coursed down Harper's face and she moaned in pain. She rolled over, onto her back, and wailed.

"Mama! Mama!" she cried. Only, her mother couldn't hear her; she was still a few miles away. The night took hold of the day, and the moon glowed in the sky, a pale orange tint emanating from space.

"It's a blood moon," a voice said several yards away.

Harper's tears stopped immediately, and she sat up in search of the voice. From across the street, a tall man, as tall as the moon itself, stood in the shadows with his hands in his pockets. She knew better than to never talk to strangers, but maybe he could help her? Drive her home? Surely, he had to know who her parents were; everyone knew the Goldens.

"Are you hurt?" he asked.

Harper's lip quivered, and she nodded. The man walked across the street, his gait slow and steady. He pulled something out of his pocket, but Harper couldn't quite see what it was. Until it reflected the light of the moon and she realized this man, this stranger, held a knife in his hand.

She backed away despite her bloody palms and crawled into the dewy grass behind her. Thunder rumbled. A flash of lightning ignited the sky. Her bicycle wheel spun from the fall, the bike still on its side.

"How old are you, little girl?" the man asked with a toothy grin.

"Ten," she answered quickly. "I have to go home. My mom and dad will be mad at me."

The knife glittered in the darkness and the man was only a few feet away now. She looked into his face, but it was hidden in the shadows of the evening.

"Would you like me to give you a ride home?"

Harper's hands throbbed and the scent of iron permeated the air. Her legs quivered. Harper knew she wasn't supposed to talk to strangers.

"I da-don't know," she stuttered.

"Come on, little girl," the man said. "I'll take real good care of you."

Harper's mouth went dry and her eyes expanded to the size of the moon overhead. Her entire body screamed at her to run away from this man. Something wasn't right. She sat rigidly in the grass and watched as the man, with his free hand, extended it for her to take.

Harper raised her own hand and droplets of blood fell from her palms and plopped onto the grass beside her. A few drops landed on the uneven concrete sidewalk, too. She looked down and noticed one of her pink shoes had come off. She must not have tied them as tightly as she should have. Only her left shoe remained on her foot.

The man followed her gaze and looked down to her feet as well. He chuckled, and the noise sent shivers down Harper's spine.

"Don't worry, little girl. You won't need your shoes for the ride home."

The strange man slid the knife into his back pocket, freeing himself to kneel beside Harper. She looked away, her heart racing inside her chest. The man reached for the shoe still on her foot and tugged it free. Now, both of Harper's shoes were off, and the man placed them neatly side by side in the grass. Her socks bore signs of wear and tear as they had holes in the toes and stains on the bottoms.

"Are you ready, little girl? Ready to go home?"

Harper nodded reluctantly as tears streamed down her cheeks. She allowed the man to hoist her up, and then he cradled her like a baby. He patted her back and forced her head to rest on his shoulder. He smelled foul and stale. Harper wrinkled her nose as fear coursed through her entire body.

"I want my Mama," she whined. "I want to go home!"

"Don't worry, little girl. I'll take the best care of you."

The stranger coddled Harper and carried her down the abandoned street. Her house was in the opposite direction, though. She sobbed for her mommy and daddy, but the stranger ignored her pleas. He had other plans in mind, none of which genuinely involved taking Harper to her home.

Panic soared through Harper's mind. As much as she tried, she couldn't catch her breath. She couldn't think. She wanted to scream for help. She even opened her mouth, but no sound came out. Harper was frozen in paralyzing fear.

Little did Harper or the man know, a second man hid in the shadows of the park, watching the entire scene unfold.

CHAPTER TWO

SUNDAY, OCTOBER 6, 2019

"All right, people. It's layout day. You know what that means—"

"Get your shit together or get out?" a handsome man with blonde curly hair replied.

"Exactly!" Peter Sanders said, followed by a wicked cough which left him massaging his throat. "Sorry, folks. Just a little sore throat, nothing to worry about!"

Excitement and electricity filled the air as the small staff of the *Crimson Chronicle* scurried about, checking their watches, emails, and the last-minute details from their stories of the week.

Peter stroked his mustache, as white as snow, and sipped his less-than-average coffee from the break room. "Penny?" he called to a thin woman with hair as black as night and silkier than a stick of butter.

"Yeah, boss?" She whipped around, tossing her hair over her shoulder. Her piercing green eyes met her boss's, and he smiled.

"You okay to work on the layout this week?" he asked.

"Yeah, I don't see why not. Even though I did it last week," she grumbled.

Peter stalked over to her, out of earshot from the others. "I'm sorry, Penny. You're just better at it, that's all. Last week, Jayson didn't place the ads correctly, and the Dollar General's ad fell off."

"Yeah, yeah, yeah." Penny rolled her eyes but cracked a brief smile. "Maybe someday we can afford to bring someone on to do layout full-time?"

"Yeah, let me look into that," Peter mocked.

Penny, or rather, Penelope considered Peter as a second father. Actually, he was her *only* father figure. Many years ago, around this time, Penny's father died in a fatal car accident when a drunk driver hit him and fled the scene. Peter and her father were friendly, and after his death, Peter took Penny under his wing.

Peter patted her on the back and left the room to go to his office in the back of the small building. The *Crimson Chronicle*, located on Main Street, beside the Crimson Falls police station, was a tattered older building with a faulty electric system which often made the production of the weekly newspaper tricky. But, Penny, a veteran reporter now, knew how to handle any crisis the paper may succumb to.

The attractive blond approached Penny. He glanced around. Once he felt comfortable knowing no one else on staff noticed them in the corner of the dull production room, he grazed his hand across Penny's ass. She smirked but made no effort to push him away.

"Meet at our spot after layout tonight?" he whispered into Penny's ear, sending chills down her muscular forearms.

She looked down to Jayson's left hand at the golden ring on his finger. "Will you have the time or do you have to be home?"

Jayson cleared his throat. "She knows I work late on Sundays."

Penny sighed. "I suppose we could meet up if, you know, production goes smoothly," she said airily.

Jayson peered over his shoulder, and still, their fellow reporters were busy twittering about. He leaned in so he could smell the lilac scent of Penny's hair and whispered into her ear, "I have a new trick I want to try on you tonight."

"Is that so?"

Jayson nodded and licked his lips.

"Well, then I guess you better hope production goes well so you can show me, huh?" Penny said.

Jayson patted her ass one more time and left her side to go fill his empty coffee cup. Penny stared after him and wondered how much longer their trysts would continue. It'd already been a couple of years since they'd started sneaking around, but Jayson's first child was on the way. She couldn't imagine he'd have much time for her after that.

She didn't quite mind, though. Penny, solely committed to her work, rarely cared to find the time for anything else. She lived and breathed journalism, and any other pleasure that wormed its way into her life was just an added bonus, but no disappointment when it slithered away, as they almost always did in time.

While Penny loved the *Crimson Chronicle* and her well-earned seniority, she longed for bigger and better things. A bigger city, a bigger paper, a bigger chance at nationwide recognition. Her heart ached for stories about political corruption and hard-hitting pieces involving anything but what she was writing now. Crimson Falls carried a high crime rate which only increased exponentially in October. Most of the stories were the typical, run-of-the-mill articles about murders and robberies. She wanted something more than that. And yet, Crimson Falls and the *Crimson Chronicle* were home.

After high school, Penelope enrolled in classes at the nearest community college in Riverside. She studied journalism, both print and broadcast, but print captured her heart with ease. She loved the rush of reporting on a story and writing the article before a tight deadline. It was like a race, and she'd always come in first. While studying outside of Crimson Falls, she experienced a taste for life beyond her home. It awakened a curious monster within her. She wanted more. More news. More stories. More life.

However, her mom, a single mother, was diagnosed with Multiple Sclerosis in October several years ago, around the time Penelope received her Associate's Degree in Journalism from Riverside Community College. The news hit them hard, and Penny faced a painful reality: she couldn't leave her mother all alone to fend for herself. And so, she gave up her dreams of relocating to a bigger city in pursuit of her dreams to stay in Crimson Falls, work for the *Chronicle* and take care of her mother. She even lived in her childhood home with her mother. She knew living in an apartment in town would be too far. Penny barely made enough to cover her bills, her mother's care, and the part-time nurse who visited the home while Penny was at work.

She'd blown through her savings after her mom's diagnosis, and she often lived paycheck to paycheck. Her mother loved her for it, though. As much as she didn't *want* the help, she knew she *needed* the help.

Penny checked her phone in search of any messages from her mother's nurse, Sophie, and once she confirmed no new texts or calls had come through, she put her phone away. Penny sat at the computer in the layout room. The *Chronicle* could only afford one Mac computer for layout. Therefore, only one person could work on the structuring of the weekly edition at a time. Typically, the staff rotated the job every Sunday, but Penny realized she'd probably be gifted the task full-time now as she was the best at it. Those InDesign classes at college were now a gift and a curse.

Being in charge of layout usually meant you were the last one out of the office on Sunday night, as you were the only one who could work on it and it had to be done to perfection. Otherwise, you'd be Jayson and leave off paid advertisements.

Penny glanced over to Jayson while he leaned against the wall with his coffee in hand and a boyish smile on his face. He scrolled through his emails on his phone with a careless nature. He looked up to see Penny watching him, and he winked at her.

Penny groaned, rolled her eyes, and returned her gaze to the computer. She tried to maintain an air of nonchalance around him, especially considering they were colleagues, too, but something about him caused her loins to purr when he looked at her. There was nothing particularly special about him: sure, he was handsome, but he wasn't an all-star reporter or even a decent reporter. He was newest to the staff and somehow scraped by, but Penny was drawn to him nonetheless. They'd dated in high school on and off, but it had never stayed serious.

She scrolled through the pages in the Adobe program and made a mental note of the sections needing to be filled.

"Jasper? Do you have your piece on the school play coming up at the elementary school?" Penny called to her fellow reporter, slightly older than her.

Jasper, bald and brown-eyed, turned from his laptop. "Yeah, just finishing up. I'll put it in the Google Drive in a few, okay?"

Penny nodded and tried not to glance back at Jayson who was now chatting up a freelance photographer. A twinge of jealousy caught in her throat, and she turned away. He was married, and even though she despised commitments, something about him kept her going back for more. Penny couldn't begin to count the number of times she promised herself the last time would be the real last time. But she kept going back to him. Even after seeing Jayson with his wife time and time again, she couldn't squelch the need to feel his naked body against hers, anytime, anywhere.

Jayson married an out-of-towner, which was rare for anyone in Crimson Falls. Mostly, people left the town, almost never came *to* town.

Around five o'clock, Peter emerged from his office with his chestnut pea coat around his arm. "I'm heading out, everyone. Have some plans tonight. Let me know if there's any problem with layout."

"See you tomorrow, old man," Penny called out.

Peter chuckled and made his exit. No one else dared speak to their boss like that, but Peter had a soft spot for Penny. Always had and always would. She could get away with more than anyone else on staff combined. Often, the others teased her for being a "brownnoser" or a "suck-up."

"Better a suck-up than a ghost," she'd retort. As a result of being Peter's favorite, it wasn't a surprise she got the better story pitches at the paper.

"I've gotta run an errand," Jayson said. "But, I'll be back to turn in my story, okay?" He smiled at Penny.

She sighed. Jayson was always the last one to turn in his articles for the week, but Penny didn't mind. It only meant they'd have the office to themselves on layout nights. She was able to work on the other sections of the paper while he finished up his piece.

A few of the staff members loitered, but others left the office as soon as they submitted their final articles to Penny. Then, Penny had the place to herself. She turned on her

Pandora app and chose the Smooth Electronic station. Once in the zone and focused, she opened the InDesign file and started to format this week's issue. About an hour or so passed before Jayson returned to the office.

His smile from earlier vanished as he pulled up a chair next to Penny.

"Hey," Penny said, typing away.

"Hi," Jayson replied shortly.

Penny turned to face him and noticed his left eye twitched, and his entire face was pale as a ghost.

"Everything okay?"

"Yeah, yeah," Jayson said and shook his head. A faint smile returned to his lips.

"It's just you and me now, kid," he said, returning to his playful demeanor while Penny placed Jasper's story into the space below the fold on the computer.

"Lovely," she said sarcastically, despite her heart skipping a beat.

Jayson stood behind Penny and placed his hands on her shoulders, gently digging his thumbs into her muscles and massaging her. A moan escaped Penny's lips, and her eyes rolled back. Jayson bent down and kissed the nape of her neck and nibbled on her ear.

"Please don't stop," Penny begged in a whisper.

"What else do you want, angel?"

Angel. It was what he called her in private. She secretly loved the nickname but never told him so.

"I want a lot of things, but I also have to get this layout done before the printer's deadline," Penny replied, out of breath.

Jayson spun her chair around and placed his palms on the arms of it, so he hovered over her. "Always such a hard worker. There's something else I need you to work on, though." His smile reeked of scandal and ill intentions.

Penny closed her eyes and waited for Jayson to lean in and press his lips against hers, but they didn't come. She opened her eyes again to see Jayson curiously staring at her.

"What?" she asked, taken aback.

"I love you," he said in all seriousness.

Penny's heart skipped a beat, and her jaw dropped. "You what?"

Jayson, still with his hands on the arms of the chair, repeated himself. "I love you, Penny."

A rush of confusion, exhilaration, and annoyance zoomed into her head all at once. "Take that back. You can't say that."

"Why not?" he asked and stood straight, letting go of his grip on her chair.

"Hmmm. Let's see, for one thing; you're married?" Penny tutted. "And, secondly, you are about to become a father!"

Oh, God. The kid, Penny thought. *I'm a home wrecker.*

"Jennifer will understand. She will want me to be happy."

Penny burst into acidic laughter. "Your wife will not be happy if you leave her and your unborn child for another woman. Plus, Jayson, we've talked about this! I don't want to date you."

"You just want to fuck me?" he asked poisonously.

"Well, yeah." Penny shrugged. "I just don't do relationships, and I don't want to be the reason your family is destroyed."

Jayson walked about and paced across the office floor. He ran his fingers through his sandy ringlets. "You aren't the reason, or wouldn't be, the reason my family breaks apart. I'm not in love with her anymore and she's not in love with me."

Penny stood abruptly from her chair and stalked to Jayson's desk. She whipped open a drawer, pulled out a hidden bottle of whiskey, unscrewed the top, and swigged.

"And how do you know that, exactly?"

Just then, Penny's phone rang from her back pocket, and she reached to answer it. Jayson shot her a look of daggers as she put the phone to her ear.

"Hello?" Penny asked with annoyance in her voice. "Seriously? Are you sure? Okay, I'll be there."

Penny returned the cell phone to her back pocket and reached for her leather jacket on the back of her chair.

"What is it?" Jayson asked, now less confrontational. "Is it your mom?"

"No," Penny sneered. "A little girl was kidnapped. Jasper just called to tell me."

"Kidnapped? Who?" Jayson asked desperately.

"The Goldens' girl, Harper," she replied.

Penny stalked out of the office with her keys in hand.

"Wait, where are you going?" Jayson called after her.

"To report on a real story. Be a doll and finish the layout for me?" Penny said.

Jayson stood there, his mouth agape, as Penny left the *Chronicle* and left him in charge of putting the rest of the issue together for print.

CHAPTER THREE

SUNDAY, OCTOBER 6, 2019

Penny dove into her used Ford Focus. The engine sputtered a few times before starting up. She heaved a sigh of relief and knew it wouldn't be long until she'd need to buy a new car. Or, rather, a newer used car.

Seeing as everyone was mostly aware of everything else in town, Penny knew where the Goldens lived. They'd bought one of the more beautiful houses in town after their law practice picked up. Penny estimated she'd be at their home in less than five minutes.

She thought back to leaving Jayson at the office with the responsibility of finishing the layout, and she smirked. She'd caught a break and a chance to report on a hot story before any of the other reporters could sink their teeth into it. Maybe, just maybe, her byline would be recognized state-wide, and she'd get a chance for some real exposure. Maybe another paper would offer her a job, one that paid more than just the minimum wage. She'd be able to move out of the God-forsaken Crimson Falls and take her mama with her. Penny salivated at the thought of recognition and a raise.

As predicted, Penny arrived at the Goldens' in less than a

handful of minutes. She frowned, having to park several houses down, as the police and other residents blocked the driveway in front of their residence. Nosey neighbors craned their necks and attempted to see inside the house while two officers stood outside, keeping the miniature mob at bay.

Penny pulled out the crumbled lanyard from her purse and tossed it around her neck. The badge read, *Crimson Chronicle Staff*, juxtaposed to a small and grainy picture of Penny taken years ago. In the photo, she appeared bright-eyed and friendly, donning a gorgeous smile filled with anticipation. Over the years, her smile waned, and the sparkle in her eyes diminished. A lackluster career had that effect on people.

Penny stepped out of her vehicle, rusted around the doors, and locked it behind her. She pushed past Crimson Falls residents bundled up with coats and scarves, eager to fight the cold for the bit of gossip lingering in the air.

"Excuse me," Penny huffed, and she squeezed through. "Move, please!"

Several people sneered at her presence and refused to move. It was then that Penny gave up on niceties and plowed through the crowd until she came face-to-face with the officers posted in front of the garage.

She recognized them both, as she did with all those in the law enforcement department. Which wasn't a difficult task: there were less than five of them in the whole town.

Penny batted her lashes and smiled brightly. "Hi, Officer Truman. I was hoping to get a statement from Chief Chapman about the missing girl."

The officer grumbled and crossed his arms. "He's inside with the parents now."

"Oh, no problem at all! I can wait," Penny offered, grinning.

The second officer rolled his eyes. "It might be a while."

"No worries. I have all the time in the world," Penny said.

Officer Truman looked her up and down, and his gaze faltered on Penny's cleavage which she had purposely left exposed in the hope of increasing her chances to speak with Darrell Chapman, head of the department.

Penny was a strong and independent woman who never let a man control her, but she didn't mind using her assets to try to control *them*. She'd learned the hard way over the years: politeness doesn't get you a story, but fierce tenacity will. No matter what the cost.

The officer peeled his eyes away long enough to extract his walkie-talkie from his belt. "Hey, uh, Chief? Penelope Waterman is out here waiting to speak with you."

Penny bowed in gratitude to the officers. Behind her, the neighbors pushed each other, eagerly hoping to hear more of what was going on inside the house. Children clung to their parents while the adults twittered about.

"She probably just ran off," one woman with rollers in her hair suggested.

"Did they search the parks yet? I bet she's there!" another cried.

Penny shook her head. *Idiots*, she thought.

The cool night air swept over those outside and the moon hung low in the sky. Electricity coursed through the air as though the president was in town. Penny pulled out her cell phone and tested her recording app to ensure its ability to perform properly when the chief was ready to speak with her.

"I'm going to be here a while longer," Chapman's gruff voice responded on the walkie-talkie.

Before the officer could reply, Penny seized the walkie-talkie and responded herself. "Hi, Chief. It's Penny. If I could just come in for a few moments, I'll be on my way and out of your hair."

Truman narrowed his eyes and forcefully grabbed the device back from her. Penny crossed her fingers inside her coat pocket and waited for the chief to respond. Her heart thumped inside her chest at the idea of a hot story just close enough for her to touch.

A rumbled groan echoed through the walkie-talkie. "Fine, let her in."

Penny stopped herself from smiling too broadly as Truman escorted her inside the house. The neighbors cried and chanted in disgust from the edge of the driveway. Before entering the house, Penny looked back and winked.

Inside the Goldens' home, a small crystal chandelier hung in the foyer and the glow of a warm house emanated throughout. Cinnamon and apples permeated the air as several candles flickered from the living room and dining room. However, despite the comforts inside, it also felt empty and devoid of happiness.

Mrs. Golden sat at the kitchen table with her head in her hands and her body convulsing with wretched sobs. Mr. Golden sat beside her and rubbed his wife's back, his face equally as swollen and distraught.

Chapman, in his early fifties with short gray hair and a hefty mustache, approached Penny with a stern look upon his face. "You have five minutes, and that's all. Got it, Waterman?"

"Of course, sir. I just need a few quotes and background information for my story."

Chapman grunted and led her to the kitchen. Penny quickly slipped off her knee-high pleather boots and tiptoed after the chief. She pulled out her phone and pressed 'record' immediately, so as to not miss a beat.

"Mr. Golden? Mrs. Golden? I'm Penelope Waterman with the *Crimson Chronicle*. I'm here to ask you a few questions about your daughter."

Mrs. Golden looked up, and Penny nearly jumped back. Her eyes, completely bloodshot, stared at her loathingly. "Why are you here?"

Penny didn't waver. "I'm so sorry about your daughter. The town will want to know what has happened and how they can help."

"You're a vulture here to pick our bones for a story," she seethed.

She's not wrong.

"If I can just have a few minutes of your time, I'll be on my way. We will do everything we can at the *Chronicle* to help you find your daughter. Maybe even a bigger paper will pick up the story. The more exposure, the better."

Mrs. Golden bit her lip and tossed aside a stray hair out of her face. "All right," she said, conceding.

"If I may?" Penny nodded toward the empty chair at the kitchen table.

Mr. Golden nodded and pulled out the chair for her. Penny sat down and put her phone in the center of the table beside three empty plates and unused silverware. On the counter lay three chicken breasts and a bag of red potatoes, neither prepared nor touched.

"Tell me what happened today. When did you last see or talk to your daughter, Mr. and Mrs. Golden?"

Mrs. Golden sat straight up and blew her nose into a tissue. Mr. Golden continued to rub her back, a stiff expression across his face.

"Well, earlier today—"

"What time would that be?" Penny interjected.

"Noon? Maybe? Well, Harper wanted to go to her friend's house. Lillian's. She knows the rule is to be home before the street lamps come on, but she never came home." Sandy Golden sniffed and blew her nose again.

"I see," Penny began. "Have you talked to Lillian's parents?"

Before Sandy or Kyle Golden could answer, Chapman spoke first. "We've talked to them, and they confirmed Harper left just before they served dinner. About two hours ago."

Penny nodded. "What do *you* think has happened, Mrs. Golden?"

"She knows to be home before the streetlights come on. She knows it!" Sandy repeated, succumbing to a new round of sobs.

Kyle Golden sighed and pardoned himself and his wife from the table. He stood and led Sandy down the hall to what Penny assumed was their bedroom. Sandy's wailing reverberated off the delicate papered walls and only softened when Kyle closed their bedroom door behind her. He returned to the kitchen with a frown and a slow gait.

"I'm sorry. Harper is our only child," he said with a shrug.

"No need to apologize, Mr. Golden," Penny said.

"Please, call me Kyle. Mr. Golden is my father."

Chapman took the vacant seat at the kitchen table in between Kyle and Penny. He took out his own notepad and scanned the scribbled details across the pages. Outside, rain descended from the dark sky and pounded against the windows. The wind howled and swirled, ripping leaves off the trees in a cascade of reds, yellows, and oranges.

"Kyle, what do you think has happened to Harper?" Penny asked carefully.

"The only thing I can think of is that she was running late and knew she wouldn't be home before the street lamps came on. Maybe she's afraid of getting into trouble, and she's hiding somewhere? I honestly don't know." A single tear slithered down Kyle's cheek.

Penny turned to Chapman. "Chief, what is your department doing to find Harper?"

Chapman stiffened and cleared his throat. "We have volunteers looking around the town, searching backyards and the playgrounds," he said. "We are putting one hundred percent of our resources on it."

"Correct me if I'm wrong, but isn't it protocol to wait twenty-four hours before a child is technically declared missing?"

"That is correct, but under the circumstances, we have decided to label her as missing as of an hour ago," Chapman said, sneering.

Penny knew of the circumstances Chapman spoke of. She glanced over to the calendar hanging just above the Goldens' landline. October thirteenth was next week.

"Do you think someone has taken Harper?" Penny asked.

More tears rushed down Kyle's face. "I hope not. But, if they did, I'd beg them to bring her back to us. Harper is our little girl, our only child, the light of our lives. We love her more than words could ever begin to describe. Our hearts are aching right now."

On the outside, Penny remained somber and empathetic. On the inside, however, she gushed, knowing Kyle had just given her an incredible quote for the story.

Kyle clutched his chest and put his head in his hands again. His body quaked against the kitchen chair, and his distraught cries sent shivers down Penny's back. She had no idea what it felt like to lose a child, but she did know what it felt like to constantly worry about losing her mother. Different types of loss, both significant and horrific. She felt torn at the moment. Half of her yearned for the story; the other half did feel sorry for the man crumbling before her.

Penny noticed the annoyance in Chapman's eyes as he watched her. "Just one more thing, Kyle. If you don't mind, do you have a photo of Harper we can use for the article? Maybe someone will recognize her?"

Kyle whimpered but pulled himself up and strode to the dining room. Chapman covered the microphone on Penny's phone and hissed to her. "It's time you ought to be leaving now, Miss Waterman."

"I know. I will leave in just a minute," she confirmed stiffly.

Kyle returned with Harper's school photo. The strawberry-blonde girl smiled at the camera with a missing incisor and a face full of freckles. Penny couldn't help but smile at the photo and take in the innocence and joy of the girl staring back at her.

"Thank you for your time, Mr. Golden. Uh, I mean, Kyle," Penny said. "I'll make sure to get this photo back to you after we scan it into our computer for printing."

Kyle nodded while Chapman stood and followed Penny to the door where she slipped into her boots and reached for the doorknob.

"I hope it was worth it," Chapman said with a growl. "You sure riled up those poor parents!"

Penny didn't turn around but opened the door and stepped out into the dreary October night.

It was so worth it, she thought.

Penny jogged to her car and raced back to the station. She had a front-page article to write and the deadline quickly approached.

CHAPTER FOUR

MONDAY, OCTOBER 7, 2019

S unlight squeezed through the dusty blinds as several crows crooned in the maple tree outside of Penny's window. She stretched while simultaneously yawning and felt her muscles tighten as her toes brushed the edge of her twin bed. She rubbed her eyes and flicked the yellowish crust from the tips of her fingers. After a moment, Penny's alarm on her phone sounded and she slapped the phone's screen while it lay on the nightstand beside her. She never needed an alarm: her body's natural cadence woke her up like clockwork every single day.

Her heart thudded in her chest as she realized copies of the *Crimson Chronicle* were being delivered to the townspeople this very moment. Soon, they would read her above-the-fold article on the front page and see her name under the photograph she'd snapped with her phone of the crowd outside the little girl's home.

Adrenaline coursed through her veins and Penny wished to be a fly on the wall of every Crimsonian's house as they read her story. However, once Penny sat up in bed and pulled her tangled hair into a messy bun, she knew other important tasks would stand in the way of her glory this morning. She needed to tend to her mother.

Penny swept her legs over the side of her bed and nuzzled her feet into her knit slippers. She pulled a black silk robe over her Nirvana tee and yellow pajama shorts, which revealed more skin than some pieces of lingerie. Penny stalked out of her room, and even though she pined for a hot cup of coffee, she needed to see her mama first.

Penny walked into her mother's room and smiled gently as the woman who brought her into the world returned her smile. Kari Waterman, former beauty queen turned librarian, passed down her good looks to Penny, but more than anything in the entire world, she hoped she wouldn't pass down her disease.

"Mornin', Ma. How did you sleep?" Penny asked as she scooted to her mother's bedside and lifted Kari's frail body up into a sitting position.

Kari nodded and smiled.

"What are you thinking for breakfast this morning? Eggs? Bacon?"

Kari shook her head and her smile faded. Penny scratched her head.

"Cereal?"

Kari shook her head again.

"We don't have much else, Ma. I haven't had a chance to go to the store yet. How about some oatmeal?" Penny suggested.

Kari nodded, and her smile returned.

"Great. Now let's get you up, okay?"

First, though, Penny smoothed away the stray gray hairs from her mother's face and stroked her cheeks. Kari closed her eyes blissfully and her body noticeably relaxed. Despite losing her father young, Penny's mother held their family together with an unshakable determination Penny admired to this day.

At Christmas, Kari showered Penny with more gifts and even bought her her first typewriter. They chopped down real Christmas trees together to find the holiday spirit and made hot cocoa every night while watching a different favorite Christmas film. No, Kari wouldn't let her daughter suffer after the death of Penny's father and her husband. In fact, the mother-and-daughter bond grew exponentially after Malcolm's accident. All they had were each other, and they formed an unbreakable chain, woven between their hearts and souls. Nothing would separate them or crush their spirits, not even Multiple Sclerosis.

Penny promised herself after her mother's diagnosis that she would borrow Kari's grit and confidence to return the favor of love and caring. She wouldn't let her mother suffer if she could help it. Every morning, she dressed her mother, served her breakfast, took her on a walk around the block, and read to her before the day nurse came in to take over while Penny headed to work. Every night, except layout night, Penny cooked dinner for herself and Kari and they watched a movie or binged a new show. They were as thick as thieves, no doubt about it.

Penny supported her mother and all of her whopping ninety pounds as she helped her to the bathroom and sat her upon the pristine toilet seat. Penny politely looked away while her mother emptied her bladder into the bowl, tinkling against the surface. Once her mother finished, Penny balled up a wad of toilet paper and helped clean her mother's behind.

At first, Penny's stomach dropped when her mother lost her mobility. She'd have to take her mother to the bathroom and wipe her? She wanted to help her mother, of course, but wouldn't it be embarrassing for both of them? But, before

Kari lost her ability to speak without an unimaginable stutter, she reminded her daughter she did the very same for her as a baby. Life had come full circle.

Next, Penny picked out her mother's outfit for the day: a pair of sweatpants and a *Crimson Chronicle* tee shirt. The previous summer, Peter put Jayson in charge of ordering shirts for the summer picnic and unfortunately, Jayson ordered one hundred instead of ten. There were still boxes at the office of the white tees with the paper's emblem blazing on the front. However, Penny took a handful of them to bring home to her mom. They were printed on a soft cotton material, which was perfect for her. And, Kari could wear one every day for weeks, and Penny still wouldn't have to do a load of laundry, if she didn't want to, that was.

While Penny made breakfast, which consisted of oatmeal and freshly squeezed orange juice, Kari sat in her wheelchair by the sliding back door. She gazed outside at the colorful leaves whipping around in the October wind. The sun livened the colors of the fallen leaves and the scene in their backyard couldn't be prettier if Monet painted it himself.

Penny's phone buzzed in her pocket and she pulled it out to see Peter's name on the Caller ID.

"Mornin'," she answered brightly.

"Who told you to go interview the parents of that girl last night?" Peter quipped.

Penny stood frozen in the kitchen, a handful of blueberries in her other hand. She furrowed her brow and her entire body stiffened. "No one. I got a lead and followed through. What's gotten into you today?" she asked sourly.

"I got an angry call from the parents this morning, that's what's gotten into me today."

Penny sighed and tossed the ripened berries into the two bowls of oatmeal on the stove. "Sorry, Peter, but the story needed to be written. A little girl is missing—"

"I know very well what's happening and I don't want any more coverage on it. Media coverage will only embolden the perp," he said with a terse finality.

"But—"

"No, buts. That is an order. Our town doesn't need any more bad news," he said.

Penny grimaced, and anger rose in her belly, bubbling like a beast with a vengeance. Over the years, several girls disappeared around this time. No one knew why and no one ever found out why. Most of the town figured the girls just ran away. After all, no bodies ever turned up.

Many years ago, when Penny was still a girl, herself, a child disappeared, one of many. Stacy Hutchings, a girl a few years older than Penny, vanished in the middle of the night. No one knew how or why. Her disappearance set the town into a frenzied panic. Mothers refused to let their kids out of the house and Penny couldn't stop wondering what happened to Stacy. Did she run away? Was she taken?

Penny wanted to press the issue with her boss but bit her tongue instead. She decided, though, she wouldn't stop investigating. Say, if Peter were to change his mind, Penny would be locked-and-loaded with a story in hand. And to continue the reporting, Penny would join the search party for Harper taking place in less than an hour.

———

DOZENS OF TOWNSPEOPLE arrived for one of two search party organizations. One group of people would search the wooded area by the cemetery and others would look on the opposite side of town near River Road in the lush area of more trees and shrubbery.

She left home once her mother's day nurse arrived with smiles and pleasantries.

"Have a good day, Miss Penny."

"You, too, Sophie," Penny replied as she kissed her mom's forehead and reached for her keys.

Penny chose to join the search party near the cemetery. This area of Crimson Falls was home to some of the less-affluent citizens, while the wealthier citizens lived on the other side of town.

A few older women stood at the front of the gathering point with packages of bottled water, crisp apples, and umbrellas. Dark clouds loomed overhead, promising another storm in the near future. The wind rattled the trees, ripping away what few leaves remained.

Standing with the women was a familiar face which caused the oxygen to disappear from Penny's lungs: Jennifer Owens.

Jennifer waved emphatically to Penny, and she wondered if the pregnant woman knew about her husband's trysts with her after hours in the newspaper office. And, yes, she cringed when she found out Jayson married a woman named Jennifer. Jennifer and Jayson Owens. The ideal couple except for the fact he'd been more unfaithful than faithful throughout their entire marriage.

Jennifer's skin glowed against the drab October sky, her face flawless and angelic. Her long, dark hair hung in a loose French braid almost to the small of her back. She was an interior decorator, soon to be a stay-at-home mother once their little one arrived.

"Penny!" Jennifer cooed with natural grace and excitement.

"Jennifer," Penny said with less enthusiasm but a toothy grin nonetheless.

"So happy you're here. Are you, uh, reporting on the search party?"

Several townspeople craned their necks in their direction,

and Penny tried her best not to scoff and roll her eyes. "Not today. Just here for the good of the community."

"Of course, of course!" Jennifer protectively rubbed her protruding belly.

Penny kicked the dirt around her faded black Converse sneakers. "Is Jayson coming, too?"

"Oh no! He's working on a story," Jennifer said. Then, she turned around to greet an older woman with frizzy white hair and too much blush.

Penny snickered to herself. Jayson hadn't been assigned a new story yet for the week. None of them have. Peter appointed stories on Tuesdays. So, wherever Jayson was at the moment, he'd lied to his wife about it. Penny couldn't help but wonder where Jayson could be, though. Usually, she assumed, he only lied to Jennifer when he was with her. So, where could he be now?

Chief Chapman stepped out of his police cruiser and trudged toward the dozens of people in the clearing.

"All right, folks. We all know why we're here. Let's split into groups of three or five and see if we can find this little girl. Shall we?"

CHAPTER FIVE

B lack. All black. No glimmer of hope hiding in the cracks of the cold concrete where Harper lay, unconscious. Not even her strawberry-blonde tendrils stood out against the blackness of the basement. Harper stirred, but barely. She stretched her short legs and feeble arms only to be greeted with the clangs of rusted chains chattering in the silence.

With each tug against the metal, Harper's sleep dissipated and fear struck through her to her very core. She opened her eyes and yet it was as if they were still closed. She couldn't see anything — not one single thing. Her chest rose and fell rapidly as she pulled against her cold, metallic restraints. Harper's hands slipped as the dried blood made it difficult to hold onto them. Her stomach grumbled, and her tongue moved around her mouth, looking, searching desperately for water. She opened her mouth to call for help, but a croak screeched into the quiet instead.

She tried as best as she could to clear her throat, but the lack of a drink caused a scratchy feeling the little girl couldn't seem to shake.

"Help!" she whispered. Then, "Someone, please help!" she called louder.

What minimal strength she possessed exploded in her chest as she wrestled the handcuffs keeping her hostage in the basement. The clanging of the metal cuffs smacking against a metal pole rang loudly. If her captor didn't know she was awake, well, now he would.

"Help!"

Tears streamed from her eyes, and instinctively, her tongue reached for them as they slid down her cheeks.

"Please! Help me!" she cried out. "My name is Harper! Help me!"

She held her breath and listened for the sound of foot- steps overhead or the ringing of sirens in the distance coming to rescue her.

Nothing.

Silence.

Only her shallow breathing made a sound.

Harper closed her eyes as the feeling of keeping them open and still seeing nothing caused nausea to boil up in her gut. She squeezed them tightly closed and imagined her mother reaching out to help her, to save her. Only it was just her imagination. Her mother wasn't here. Her mother couldn't save her.

Harper thought back to hours ago, at least she thought it'd only been a few hours when she fell off her bike, and the stranger pretended to help her. Instead, he stole her. He heaved her ineffectual body over his shoulder and plucked her from the Earth like a child ripping dandelions out of the ground on a warm spring day.

Her stomach grumbled, and Harper reached for her aching side. Despite being kidnapped and terrified for her life, the little girl's appetite roared inside of her. She needed something to eat. Some kind of sustenance. Anything. She'd even willingly eat the meatloaf from school if it was offered to her, despite the questionable ingredients. Even vegetables sounded appetizing. Anything.

Harper continued to pull against her restraints despite knowing her efforts were fruitless. She called for her mother over and over again, but she didn't come.

The man who took her last night said he was trying to save her, but from what? Harper didn't know. All she knew was the man kept calling her by a different name: Heather.

"That's not my name," Harper whispered in the stranger's truck.

"Don't look at me," he grumbled.

Stale coffee and cigarettes permeated the air inside the truck, and Harper gagged on the harshness of it. But, she listened to the man and didn't dare look at him. In fact, she thought if she did, she'd be staring into the eyes of the Boogie Man himself. She didn't want to see that, no way, no how.

More tears poured down Harper's cheeks as she clutched her belly. She wished more than anything her parents could hold her right now and save her, make her feel safe. Thunderstorms terrified Harper and every time one hit, her mom or dad would pull her into their lap and soothe her by twirling her hair between their fingers. Sometimes, they pulled on her tangles unintentionally. Most of the time, the storm canceled out her crying.

"It's just Jesus bowling with his friends," her mother promised.

Harper would bite her lip and stare into the menacing clouds, wondering if this was true.

"But, how do you know?" she'd ask.

"I just know, love," her mom would reply.

When fear overwhelmed Harper to the point she could barely breathe, she tried to remember the story her mom told her about the bowling. She clung to it like a life preserver. Even if it was just a story, it provided a tiny ray of hope.

What would her mother tell her now? What reasoning or story would she give about the man who took her from the park and locked her up like an animal?

"Mama!" Harper cried "Help me!"

As Harper wept for her parents and begged God or Jesus or whoever was in charge of Heaven, footsteps pounded overhead. Harper's breath caught in her throat, and she stopped crying. Her body turned rigid, and she pushed her back up against the cool stone wall behind her. She didn't move; she didn't blink.

The steps grew louder and louder until they stopped. Harper craned her neck to listen for her captor. Or, was it someone here to save her? To rescue her? She couldn't breathe but dug her nails into the palms of her hands, desperately waiting.

A doorknob turned, the sound screeching through the silence of the basement. A man cleared his throat and stepped down the basement stairs — one at a time.

Thump.

Thump.

Thump.

More tears leaked from Harper's eyes and snaked down her face. If there were light in the basement, it would be clear to see her tears streaked through the dirt covering the child's cheeks.

The man reached the bottom step, and the door swung shut, ripping away the short connection from the basement to the outside world.

Harper squeezed her eyes shut but sensed a faint light in the room now. Maybe the man brought a flashlight? Or used his phone for light as she often saw her mother do during dark mornings when she tried to wake Harper for school without turning on the bright princess lights of her room.

The man's odor swelled and filled the room: sweat and cigarettes. But, this time, Harper smelled something else, too.

"Hiya, Heather. You hungry?"

CHAPTER SIX

MONDAY, OCTOBER 7, 2019

P enny slipped a crisp Grant toward the greasy teen boy managing the front desk at the Haven Inn. He flicked his head to the side so his chin-length dyed-black hair wouldn't be in his eyes. He nodded politely at Penny and put his head down, pocketing the bill.

The boy, Jeremy, was used to Penny paying for a room by the hour without putting her name on any register or sign-in sheet. She didn't tell him what she needed the room for, and he didn't ask. It was nice that way, easier. She didn't want any hard evidence or records of her rendezvous at the Haven.

Penny strode up the single flight of stairs and opened room 204, her usual. She kicked off her boots, now soiled with dried mud, and peeled her baggy black t-shirt over her head. She still had fifteen minutes.

Even though she planned on taking a shower before leaving the room, hot water against her back called to her, so she decided to take one now, too. She had the time to spare. After tossing her clothes on the second twin bed, Penny hopped into the shower and turned on the hot water. Just the hot water.

She stood under the showerhead, and a slight moan escaped her lips. Her muscles nearly sang with glee as the steaming water thrashed against her back. Many people despised this kind of overly powerful shower, but Penny lived for this kind of relaxation. A little pain, a little bliss, and the overwhelming sensation of numbness when she turned the water off.

Lost in thought, Penny hardly noticed the door to the motel room slam shut and the lock click into place. She closed her eyes; her alone time was over.

"Hey," a familiar voice said. "Why are you showering before we get dirty?"

"Hi, Jayson," Penny said. "I just needed a quick rinse."

Jayson's eyes washed over Penny's bare body, raw and red from the water pressure. He bit his lip and leaned into the tub, pulling Penny's face closer to his.

"You look gorgeous," he said, his voice barely above a whisper.

Not one to return the compliment, Penny simply closed her eyes and smashed her lips against his, losing herself in the pent-up passion building between the two. They hadn't come here in over two weeks. The tension had peaked days ago, but now they'd finally have their chance to release it.

Penny turned off the water, a little begrudgingly. Sure, she wanted to feel Jayson's touch, to touch him, but there was something about the solace of being alone that often left her more satisfied than anything. Still, she yearned for the goofy man with the curly hair hoisting her out of the tub and cradling her in his arms.

Jayson nibbled at her neck and sent Penny into a fit of laughter. He knew her sweet spot, her ticklish spot, her everything. She'd lost her virginity to him, after all. And they'd practiced plenty when they were in high school.

Once they reconnected again at the paper, it was like

riding a bike. Everything familiar and easy. She knew him, and he knew her.

Jayson carried Penny to the bed and gently tossed her on top of the ivory comforter, bitten away at places from the moths. He army crawled onto the bed too and inched toward the apple of his eye. He started at her calf and kissed his way up, higher and higher.

Penny tossed her head back in ecstasy as Jayson's tongue explored her and pleasured her. She reached for the bed frame and gripped it until her knuckles turned white.

"Jayson," she breathed.

Jayson continued to climb his way up farther and farther until his lips brushed against Penny's breasts. He nipped at her soft, pink nipples.

Penny's moans increased in volume, but she didn't care. She wouldn't deny herself the release she desperately wanted. Needed.

Finally, their mouths met again. Jayson slipped his tongue inside Penny's mouth. She tasted herself on him, and it only sent her body spiraling down and her heart to race. Opening her eyes, Penny tugged at Jayson's pants and unzipped them with ease. He ripped off his shirt, literally.

Both stopped for a moment and snickered at the torn white cotton tee on the floor. With her hands above her head, Jayson's hands slipped into hers; she was defenseless against him.

"I've missed you," Jayson whispered into Penny's ear. "I want you so badly. Do you want this, too?"

Penny nodded and stifled the desire to call out for him to keep going. "Don't stop," she breathed. The sheets dampened underneath Penny's body. From the shower to the perspiration between them.

As requested, Jayson didn't stop. He thrust himself inside

Penny as metaphorical fireworks exploded between them. They held each other's gaze and rocked back and forth. Feeding off each other's pleasure, wanting to give the other more and more.

———

JAYSON STOOD by the window with his pants on but unzipped. He didn't bother putting his shirt back on. He gazed into the blustery night with a lit cigarette hanging limply outside his mouth.

"That's a nasty habit," Penny chided.

"It helps me calm down after incredible sex," he said with a wink.

Penny rolled her eyes. It was routine for Jayson to have a Marb Red after sex. He did it every time, despite her pleas for him to quit or at least not smoke around her.

"I like clean air, and you know, not getting cancer," she once said.

"We're all going to die someday," he'd replied.

Jayson inhaled deeply and exhaled outside of the motel window. Despite his best efforts, though, some of the smoke eased back into the room. Penny wrinkled her nose and sprayed an extra spritz of perfume on the nape of her neck. She changed into jeans and a hoodie, no longer needing a professional façade.

"I saw your wife today," she said.

Unfazed, Jayson turned around. "Oh, yeah? How'd that go?"

"Fine. We were in the same group for the search party," Penny said.

Jayson nodded. "She said she was going to that thing today."

Penny slipped into her black combat boots and laced

them up. Her hair dripped down her neck and onto her back, dampening her t-shirt.

"Why didn't you go?" Penny held her breath.

"I, uh, had other things to do," he said and shrugged.

Penny narrowed her eyes. "Other things? Like what?"

"Quite the little reporter, are we?" Jayson whistled.

"Just curious is all. The entire town is out looking for a little girl and your wife shows up without you on her arm." Penny's cheeks reddened.

"Don't worry about it, okay? It doesn't concern you," Jayson snipped, a touch of poison seeping through his words. "And, besides, it's not like this town hasn't dealt with a missing kid before."

"Hmmm. Okay. A little girl goes missing, and you don't seem to care. Best dad of the year award right here, huh?"

She couldn't understand why he didn't seem to care more about Harper's disappearance, considering he'd suffered a similar situation. During high school, not too long after they started dating, Jayson's little sister disappeared. At first, the police pursued Jayson as the top suspect. It was known to many that Jayson and Shannon argued more than what seemed normal for siblings.

Even Penny noticed their heated sibling rivalry. She assumed it was the age difference; Jayson in high school and Shannon in elementary school.

Luckily, he had an alibi. The night Shannon disappeared, Jayson had taken Penny to the movies. While no one at the theatre remembered them, Jayson found the stub. He showed it to the police who then backed off. Shannon was never found and despite his alibi, many people in Crimson Falls believed he had something to do with it. He never talked about Shannon, but every October, the anniversary of her disappearance, whispers followed him wherever he went.

Still, Penny thought Jayson might show a little interest in

finding Harper, considering his own sister never returned to Crimson Falls.

Penny collected the rest of her belongings, and without another word to Jayson, she stalked out of the room and let the door slam behind her. She wasn't exactly sure what he was hiding, but she'd be damned if she didn't do everything in her power to find out.

CHAPTER SEVEN

TUESDAY, OCTOBER 8, 2019

The next morning, Penny and her mother ventured through the usual routine before the day nurse arrived. However, Penny's mind was plagued with questions from the night before. What was Jayson hiding? Why didn't he care more about Harper's disappearance? Surely, as a soon-to-be father himself, it should have some impact on him? What if one of his children were kidnapped?

Shaking away the dark thoughts, Penny kissed her mother goodbye and headed toward the office. On the drive, Penny noticed nearly all the light and utility poles in town were covered with missing posters of Harper. Penny's heart sank. Harper was more than a juicy story, a chance for a byline above the fold. She was a real person, a little girl gone missing. She had a family who loved her and wanted nothing more than to hold her in their arms again.

As much as she tried to keep up the frosty walls around her heart, the face of the little strawberry-blonde girl smiling back at her every several feet thawed it a bit. Instinctually, she wanted to help find the girl, and not just for the story, but to reunite a family.

What has come over me? she thought.

Penny could only assume her contrasting reaction derived from the fear of what it would feel like to lose her mother. Or, how her mom would feel if she lost Penny.

The only problem in helping investigate the case? Her boss stood firmly in her way.

"Good morning, team," Peter said with bright eyes and a broad smile.

"Mornin'," the staff grumbled as they sipped their mediocre coffee around a tattered table in the office.

"It's that time again. Time to pick our stories for the upcoming week," Peter said enthusiastically.

Penny sat across from Jayson who refused to meet her gaze. Despite his distance, Penny stared at him, waiting, daring him to look back at her. She wanted him to know she was curious about the mysterious aura he threw on like a jacket so suddenly last night, shielding him from her questions. But, he wouldn't give in. Instead, he stared at his notepad or kept his focus firmly on Peter.

"Anyone have ideas they'd like to pitch?"

Jasper raised his hand like an attentive school girl. "I have one!"

"Go on," Peter said.

"There's a mural going up on the side of The Crooked Crow down the street. They hired someone from out-of-state to paint a map of Crimson Falls," Jasper replied proudly.

"Excellent! I'd like to get quotes from the owner, name, and the artist. And, don't forget a photo of the progress," Peter instructed.

Jasper saluted their boss and scribbled furiously on his notepad. Penny rolled her eyes; Jasper was always one for sucking up. Even so, she didn't have any ideas for the upcoming edition of the *Crimson Chronicle*. Deep in her heart, she assumed Harper's disappearance would keep her busy for weeks, but she doubted it was the right time or place to bring it up in their staff meeting. Especially considering her and Peter's heated phone conversation from the day before.

"The high school is having their annual talent show this Friday. I could do that," Jayson suggested.

"Wonderful. You're on it. Bring a camera, as I'm sure you know we'll want some close-ups and action shots of the acts."

Jayson nodded and proceeded to write down a few notes on his own pad of paper donning the *Crimson Falls Chronicle* logo at the top.

As the meeting progressed, Peter assigned a few more pieces to the other staff members, including a few robberies overnight, a vandalized home near the cemetery, and a domestic dispute by the school. Then, as though a spotlight was purposely directed onto her, Peter looked to Penny with a surveying gaze.

"What about you, Penny? What will you be writing about this week?"

His voice almost challenged her to say something about the missing girl. She knew better, though, than to address the situation in front of her colleagues. Instead, she searched her brain frivolously for something, anything she could pitch.

"I'm still waiting for some stories to progress enough to write about them," she said, her voice with a slight strain. "But, I thought I could assist Jayson at the talent show. You know, instead of a single article, make it a spread."

She bit her lip as she watched her boss ponder the idea. Would he take the bait? And, for the first time during the meeting, Jayson turned to look at Penny, a menacing glare etched across his usually cherub-like façade.

"Sure, why not?" Peter said. "Then, with a few more ads, we'll have no problem filling up space. Great work, everyone. Now, get to writing!"

With that, the staff meeting was adjourned. While the others shuffled out of the room and meandered toward the break room for more coffee, Jayson pulled Penny aside and out of earshot.

"What was that about?" he sneered.

"What was what about?" Penny shrugged, feigning a sense of naivety.

"You know what," Jayson hissed. "I don't need you to help me cover the freakin' talent show."

"It could be fun," Penny said with a grin.

Jayson huffed and stalked away to his desk, further proving to Penny he had something to hide. But, what could it be? Doubt etched itself into her mind, deep in the folds of her thoughts and the truths she'd clung to all these years. Jayson had always been a good guy, minus the affair, but he wasn't a bad man. Had something changed?

Penny glanced outside the window and a glossy poster with Harper's face and home phone reflected under the October sunlight. A pang of sadness radiated within Penny's gut, and she didn't think twice as she strode into Peter's office.

"Well, if it isn't my star reporter," Peter said.

"Can we talk?" Penny asked quickly.

Peter motioned her inside, and Penny closed the door behind her. She looked at her boss and noticed his cheerful demeanor had been extinguished and a melancholic ambiance took hold. The bags under his eyes were marginally more noticeable, and his smile thinned.

"Everything okay?" Penny asked.

"Oh, you know. Life," Peter replied.

Penny followed her boss's gaze toward a photograph on his desk. It was of a little girl with electric crimson hair and eyes as big as the moon. The girl sat on a swing and was missing her two front teeth.

"Today is her birthday," Peter said.

Penny lowered her head and stared at her black combat boots. Her boss rarely mentioned his late daughter. In fact, Penny didn't know much about her at all except for the fact she died many years ago from a horrible accident.

"I'm very sorry, Peter," Penny said.

She walked over to her boss, around his desk, and put her chin on his shoulder, wrapping her arms around him, too. Penny could almost feel the despair radiating off Peter, the emptiness, the devastation. It doesn't matter how much time passed after losing a loved one; the heartache would forever leave its furious claws in your heart.

Peter patted Penny behind him, and his face softened. "You would have loved her. I bet you two would have been the best of friends."

"I'm sure we would have," Penny said.

Peter cleared his throat. Penny let go of her boss, ending their father-daughter embrace. "So, uh, what was it you wanted to talk about?"

Penny retreated to the other side of Peter's desk and sat down across from him. She, too, cleared her throat, now doubting this was the appropriate time to broach the subject.

"I was hoping to talk more about my story. The one about Harper," she said.

Suddenly, Peter's eyes darkened, and the anguish disappeared like a fire during a storm. "I thought I made myself clear about this, Penelope." He used her full name, causing Penny to cringe.

"I just thought we could discuss it a little more," she said earnestly.

"Well, you thought wrong."

A chill radiated throughout the room and Penny rubbed her forearms. "It's a big story, Peter. People will want to know what's going on with the search for her."

"Then they can ask the police!" His cheeks turned a shade of puce as his chest rose and fell wildly.

Penny shook her head. Then she looked over at the photo of his daughter on his desk. At that moment, it suddenly clicked to her: Peter didn't want to cover Harper's disappearance because it pained him too much. She probably reminded him of the loss of his own daughter.

Peter's phone rang and each of them stared at the black cradle as the red light flickered on and off. "I need to take this," Peter grumbled.

"Sure. Yeah, of course."

Penny stood and felt Peter's gaze piercing into her back as she left his office. The men in her life were driving her crazy. However, as she stepped out of Peter's office and again looked out the window to Harper's poster, she knew she couldn't let this go. Even if it wouldn't be published in the paper, even if she couldn't slap her name on it, Penny knew she had to help solve this case. No matter what the cost.

CHAPTER EIGHT
TUESDAY, OCTOBER 8, 2019

Penny parked her car in the visitor lot of the Crimson Falls High School. A surge of nostalgia coursed through her veins as she recalled her own time enrolled at the school. The high school had been a bit lonely for her: she didn't have many friends, nor did she try to make any, either. She served as the school newspaper's editor and lead reporter, but the other staff on the student-run paper mostly stayed clear of her. Often sour, she left a bad taste in many mouths. Penny cared more about reporting the truth than who she needed to trample on to finish the piece.

Many kids at school didn't understand what Jayson saw in Penny when they first started dating. Penny, herself, didn't understand at first, either. It didn't take long for her to figure it out, though. She wasn't like most girls pining after him. She wasn't a cheerleader or a popular girl. Jayson didn't want the stereotypical high school girl. He wanted something more.

She smiled while she strode across the quiet parking lot and veered toward the main entrance of the school. Threatening clouds blanketed the sky. The nearly naked trees swayed in the chilly breeze.

When Penny was a senior, she heard rumblings of a student teacher meeting some of the girls at The Crooked Crow and sneaking them in. A few even giggled and gossiped in the locker rooms before gym class about the teacher, Andrew, kissing them before the night ended. Adrenaline suffocated Penny, and she knew she had to get the full story.

During one particular gym class, Penny pretended to need one of the larger mirrors in the ladies' locker room to spruce up her makeup before class, even though she didn't wear any. She plumped and played with her cheeks while she listened to the girls in the next row talk about Andrew and swap stories of their swapping spit with the student teacher, who although wasn't too much older than them, still shouldn't have been consorting with his pupils.

The girls, still young and immature, didn't even think to be jealous of each other, but instead, felt as though they'd been invited to a secret club. They didn't mind sharing the teacher because an older man desired them. That was all that mattered.

"He told me to meet him tonight at eight," the one girl cooed while twirling her long honey-brown hair.

"Oh, my God! Do you think you'll go to second base this time?" another brainless cheerleader squawked.

"We'll see," the first girl replied.

Penny tried not to audibly gag, and instead, internalized the information and planned her stakeout for later that night.

She borrowed her mom's car and waited patiently while she watched every single person go in and out of the bar. Andrew, already balding, but with broad swimmer's shoulders, strolled up just before eight. He glanced around and over his shoulder before pulling something small out of his pocket, spraying it into his mouth, and leaned against the side of the establishment. At eight, right on cue, Melissa from school showed up, wearing a skirt as short as can be. Not to mention her cotton-candy-pink lipstick bright and loud enough for someone in an airplane to see.

Andrew pulled Melissa under his arm and kissed her forehead. This time, Penny didn't need to silence herself and pretended to gag, hidden in the darkness of the night. With her disposable Kodak camera in hand, Penny walked into the bar. There wasn't a bouncer, so she strode into the establishment with ease. Penny spotted the student-teacher couple and stalked toward them. They were huddled together at a corner table. Many patrons smoked their cigarettes, sipped their vodka sodas, and chugged Budweiser beers. She knew it was them, though. She could see Melissa's lipstick through the haze.

Without an introduction, Penny approached the table and snapped away madly at the scene before her. Before they even knew what was going on, Penny managed to get a few shots of them kissing. Andrew then looked up in horror.

"Penelope? What are you doing here?"

"Penny, you snitch!" Melissa cried.

"Just covering my next big expose for the paper. Thanks, guys. Oh, and enjoy jail, Andy. Don't drop the soap!"

Andrew stood and pushed Melissa out of the booth. Penny sensed he would follow her, and she weaved in and out of the others at the bar and ran to her mother's car. She saw Andrew standing dumbfounded in the street from her rearview mirror.

After the story spread across the school, Andrew lost his student teaching gig and his chance to ever be a teacher in the state again. Penny earned herself even more of a bad rap because all of Andrew's little club members blamed her, and rightfully so, for their boyfriend being blacklisted.

But, despite her harsh reputation, she'd managed to wrangle Jayson, the school's quarterback, all the same. Sometimes, the oddest couples made the most sense. Who would have thought, after meeting in high school, a decade or so later they'd be working at the *Crimson Chronicle* together? Definitely not Penny or anyone else in town. Jayson had acquired a full ride on a football scholarship to Notre Dame but tore his ACL during the high school championship game. It was a career-ending injury. The scholarship was revoked. Thus began his downward spiral from popular jock with the world at his fingertips to a married man, a low-paid reporter with an affair under his belt.

"Penelope!" Mr. Harden squeaked and pulled her into his arms.

"Principal Harden, it's so great to see you," Penny said with faux enthusiasm.

Mr. Harden let go of his grasp on his former student, his toupee off center and many more wrinkles gracing his face.

"So, I hear you're the one who's going to cover our talent show this year, huh?"

"Jayson and I will be covering it together, actually." Color rose to her cheeks. Penny couldn't recall how many times Principal Harden had caught the pair behind the bleachers or in the janitor's closet while at school. Even then, they'd had a propensity for sneaking around at inappropriate times.

Mr. Harden nodded, his smile fading just a touch. "Splendid. Well, shall we get started?"

She followed Mr. Harden into his office and remembered all too well making the same walk years ago after exposing Andrew and Melissa. Naturally, the principal had wanted to know everything she knew about the hush-hush goings-on in his school. He was grateful Penny gathered the information but didn't miss his chance to scold her either about publicizing it so broadly for the whole school and town to know.

Penny sat in the chair across from Mr. Harden's, a brown leather chair much fancier than the one she remembered. She pulled out her phone and opened the recording app she used for her interviews.

"Ready?" she asked.

"Say, do you know anything more about that little girl gone missing? Harper is her name?"

Penny paused the recording with a sigh. "I don't know more than what you probably know. I'm sure you read my piece in this week's edition of the paper?"

Mr. Harden nodded and stroked his beard that was speckled with more white and gray than brown, as it had been many years ago. Picture frames with images of his family covered his desk, including his three daughters who had gone to school with Penny growing up. Educational awards and diplomas hung on his walls. Penny knew in his desk, he had a drawer full of confiscated items taken from kids. Back in her day, it was mostly harmless things like a whoopie cushion or even some small Swiss army knives. She could only imagine what the kids were smuggling in these days or how many cell phones vibrated in the depths of the cherry wood desk.

"Such a tragedy," Mr. Harden said. "Do you think she's still alive?"

Penny's stomach dropped and turned wickedly. She assumed the answer but couldn't bring herself to speak it out loud. The idea of the words *probably not* lingered on her lips but wouldn't come. So, she shrugged instead.

Most of the young girls who disappeared in Crimson Falls didn't come back alive. Many weren't even found. It was an underlying rule that if you went missing, you weren't coming back.

Mr. Harden's eyes moistened. He rubbed at them with a swift flick of his wrist, trying to conceal his sudden emotions. Then, he clapped his hands and the cheerful smile from earlier returned.

"Well, then, shall we begin?"

The interview only lasted about fifteen to twenty minutes as Mr. Harden detailed the changes in this year's show, which included a new award for group acts and a freshman-only category. Penny wrapped up her questions and thanked her former principal for his time.

"Jayson should be stopping by sometime this week to interview a few more faculty members and some of the students participating this year."

"Very well," Mr. Harden said. "It was great to see you, Penelope. Don't be a stranger!"

Penny forced a smile and waved as she hurriedly swooped across the parking lot to her car. Although, with every step of the way, another massive wave of sadness washed over her at the thought that Harper may never walk this parking lot because, most likely, she wouldn't be alive for high school at all.

CHAPTER NINE

WEDNESDAY, OCTOBER 9, 2019

Time. What was time and where did it go when you had no way to track it? Without a clock in range, did time disappear? If you couldn't measure it, did it ebb and flow as it pleased?

Harper, still chained in the stranger's basement, lost all sense of where she was and how long she'd been there. It felt like months, years, maybe, since she'd last seen her parents or her friends. How long had she been a prisoner in this man's torture chamber? Was she old enough to drive yet? Old enough to date? Had time begun to move backward? Was she a little babe again, unable to care for herself, in need of a parent's touch?

With cracked and chapped lips, Harper sat in silence. That was all there ever was now. Silence. With the rare exception of the strange man bringing her little to no food and calling her by another name.

"Oh, Heather," he'd whisper. "I'm so happy to have you back."

When he visited with a small glass of water and sometimes oatmeal or soup, which Harper spilled more than she ate, his voice turned soft and sweet.

"I love you, Heather," he'd whisper.

It didn't take long for Harper to wear out her vocal cords crying for help. It did't take long for her throat to dry up and her tear ducts to do the same. She couldn't cry again if she wanted to. She had nothing left to give.

Harper slouched, unfazed as footsteps pounded overhead against the floor. She couldn't remember what the man looked like anymore, but she knew he wore heavy boots and the sound of his stomping around upstairs echoed within the chilled, stone basement below.

The man disappeared for part of the day. However, she didn't know which part it was. Did he leave for the night, or was he gone for the duration of the day? She couldn't guess if her life depended on it.

Without her sight, Harper's other senses morphed into super-sensitive capabilities. While she couldn't see, she could hear every single drop of water emitted from the sink only feet away. She could smell the metallic, bitter taste from the water, too. Urine permeated the air, but she grew accustomed to that in no time. She didn't have a choice. Harper could taste the staleness in the air and could pinpoint almost all the ingredients in the few and far between meals the man brought her.

To pass the time, Harper daydreamed about the possibility of her becoming a superhero with her new acute senses. She'd zip around the city blindfolded and rescue other kids in danger. She wouldn't need her vision to help them because she'd sense the fear in the air, hear their calls for help, smell the metallic scent of blood, and taste the adrenaline in her body. No other little boy or girl would ever suffer at the hands of evil men. She'd save them. Every last one.

The door creaked open, and a slim ray of buttery light squeezed through. Although, not enough to illuminate the basement, enough to glimpse her filthy hands folded in her lap. And only for a few moments.

"I'm coming, Heather. Are you hungry?"

"Yes. Thank you," Harper replied monotonously.

The man cleared his throat and Harper's ears pricked as she heard him rifle through his trousers for a handkerchief. He spat inside of it and stuffed it back into his pocket. Harper cringed at the thought of that dirty material inside the man's pocket. Her mother would never have allowed her to do the same.

"Harper, you can't carry around germs like that. You'll get everyone and their mothers sick!" her mama would say.

The man left the door open a crack every time he made his way down to visit Harper. He needed to be able to see where he was going, but he'd never turn on a light bulb. Only use the glow from the upstairs. Maybe he didn't want Harper to see him? Although she already had the night he took her. Maybe, just maybe, though, he didn't want to see *her.*

Harper closed her eyes as the man's footsteps shuffled closer and closer. Even though she could barely make him out, she didn't want to try. She'd only just forgotten his face and didn't want to be shocked into remembrance. Her nightmares were filled with enough monsters; she didn't need another.

With her eyes squeezed shut, she could still sense the man's moist palm reaching for her forehead.

"You're feeling warm today, Heather," he said with a gruff voice.

"Mhmmm," she said.

She'd stopped correcting him when he called her Heather. It made no use. He kept calling her the name no matter what she said or did. The question buzzing in Harper's mind, though, was who was Heather and where was she now?

"You want some soup?" he asked eagerly.

Harper nodded. "Yes, please."

Her mama taught her better than to forget her manners, no matter what the situation. Even in shackles, Harper always said *please* and *thank you*.

The aroma of a plain chicken broth filled her nostrils. Her stomach rumbled ferociously. She presumed, like the past meals, there would be a sparse amount of vegetables and chicken in the broth, but she didn't care. Any kind of sustenance was fine. She needed to keep her strength.

"All right, Heather. Tip your head back. Yes, that's it, girl," the man cooed before another fit of coughing roared through the basement.

He never unlocked her handcuffs during meal time. Instead, he helped her eat by slowly tipping the bowl of soup or oatmeal for her to drink from. The man didn't take any chances for her to escape. But there had to be a way. He'd slip up sometime, somehow, right?

The lukewarm broth scorched down her throat. Harper caught the mushy vegetables and easily mashed them with her teeth so she'd swallow them easier. She tried time after time to sip the soup slowly, so as to make it last a little longer. Even if that meant staying in the company of her captor longer. But she didn't want to finish her food too quickly. She never knew when he'd come again to feed her. She couldn't manage to keep track of the meal times. She didn't know if he came once a day, twice a day? Every other day. Time disappeared to her.

"How's the soup, Heather?" he asked as she swallowed the last gulp.

"Is there any more?" Harper held her breath. She'd never asked for more before. She didn't want to anger the man.

Fear ripped through her every time she opened her mouth to make a request and ended up biting her tongue, instead.

Silence filled the air again as though the man wasn't there at all. "Still hungry, huh? Growing an appetite?"

Harper nodded then remembered he might not be able to see her do so in the shadowy darkness of the basement. "Yes. I'm a growing girl." Her voice cracked.

The man coughed into his arm and pulled his handkerchief out again to blow his nose. "Let me see what I can come up with, okay?"

Harper's heart raced. The man, while rough and cruel, had a fatherly instinct Harper recognized. Was he a dad? Of course, her own father treated her a million times better, but she could sense a strange form of love this man had for her. Whether it was because he sang to her or told her stories from time to time, it seemed as though he might have thought she was his daughter. This Heather he spoke of, maybe she *was* his daughter?

"Thank you, Daddy," Harper said and held her breath. She was waiting to see what the man would say.

More silence.

Then he sniffled and choked up again.

"Daddy loves you so much, Heather," he said. "Let me go get my growing girl some crackers."

He pulled himself up and stumbled toward the stairs, continuing to sniffle and weep. Harper took a huge risk but trusted her instincts. If the man thought she was his daughter, could she manipulate his love for her to set her free?

Harper sat in the familiar darkness, surrounded by her thoughts, and constructed a plan in her mind. The very next opportunity she had, she would escape this place. Escape the man holding her hostage. Escape the darkness.

CHAPTER TEN

After meeting with Mr. Harden, Penny's stomach growled and reminded her she forgot to pack lunch today. She looked down to her watch and saw the shorthand kissed the twelve. Inside her car, she cruised back to the office, hoping she'd had the foresight to bring extra snacks the last time she went grocery shopping. In the confines of her old vehicle, her stomach grumbled again.

Damn, chill, she thought.

She turned onto Main Street and slowed down to accommodate the handful of pedestrians walking across the street and away from Crimson's Cookery, a petite spot with unbelievable wraps for lunch and a bakery to die for. Not literally, but close enough. After five, the menu switched over to dinner options which included home-cooked comfort food with a side of heart disease: Penny's favorite dish was the fettuccini alfredo with a side of garlic bread.

Penny patted her belly and veered right into an open parking spot in front of the restaurant, nearly knocking over a bicycle locked around a thin tree trunk planted by the main strip's sidewalk.

The aroma of fresh bread and sweet tea wafted through the air and tickled Penny's senses. Typically, she ate lunch at her desk, if she even ate at all. Outside the Cookery, vines clung to the faded and chipped paint upon the building, snaking up and down the sides. A few smaller tables and chairs were left on the patio. However, the weather around this time of the year didn't leave much to be desired for eating outside.

Penny stepped across the threshold and was greeted by the clanging of several bells on top of the door. Inside the Cookery, a few older couples and some kids, presumably either skipping school or taking advantage of their off-campus lunch privileges, sat at the vintage wooden tables. Local artwork hung beautifully on the walls, and the original tile still lay in place. The Cookery could make any patron feel like they were eating at their beloved grandparents' house: cozy, homey, and a dash of nostalgic.

"Table for one?" Stella, the hostess, asked with her foreign Southern drawl.

"Make that a table for two," a voice behind Penny chirped.

Penny's stomach dropped and not because of her appetite. She turned around to find Jayson's wife standing and looking deep into her eyes with a flicker of curiosity sparkling in the corners.

"Hey, Jennifer," Penny said awkwardly.

"I saw you walking in, and I was hoping I could join you for lunch," she said and rubbed the top of her belly, as big as a beach ball.

Penny waited a moment or two in hopes Jennifer would change her mind, but her pearly white smile said otherwise.

"Uh, yeah. Sure. Sounds good."

Stella strolled to a corner booth and stepped aside, allowing the women to scooch onto the cedar benches across from each other.

"I'll bring y'all some waters to start and let ya look at the menu," Stella said with a smile as sweet as pie.

Penny nodded and then her gaze darted down to the menu even though she knew it by heart. She stared at the menu and wished she could pry herself away from her secret lover's wife.

"What do you think you're going to get?" Jennifer asked. Penny could hear the smile in her voice.

"I'm not quite sure yet," she lied.

Jennifer folded her menu and pushed it to the end of the table with her perfectly French-manicured fingertips. She cleared her throat and Penny's heart pulsed against her chest as if it were to explode any second. Sweat collected at her temple and more dripped down her back. The breeze from the door opening and closing every few minutes felt cool against her moist tailbone.

Why did Jennifer corner Penny at the restaurant? Why did she insist they sit together when they barely socialized, even during public events? They'd never double-dated or hung out one-on-one before. Did she know? Was she going to confront her about the affair? So many questions raced through Penny's head, her appetite disappeared in the blink of an eye.

"So, I wanted to ask you something," Jennifer began slowly.

Penny gulped and looked at Jennifer's face, hoping to read her expression. Jennifer's smiled faded, and Penny noticed the massive bags under her eyes. Her makeup was smudged a little, and her mascara flaked onto her pale cheeks. Jennifer instinctively rested her hands on her belly. Penny dug her nails into the palms of her hands. Sure, she was tough, but not "sit across from a pregnant woman and admit to banging her husband" kind of tough.

"What is it?" Her voice cracked.

"You know Jayson more than almost anyone, right?"

More beads of sweat dripped down Penny's back, and she gulped. "Uh, yeah. I mean, I used to. Now, we're just colleagues mostly."

Oh my, God! Shut up, Penny! she thought.

"Do you think he's been acting strangely lately?"

Stella returned with their waters and her tiny notebook at the ready. "Can I take y'alls' order now?"

Penny exhaled; Stella brought a welcomed interruption. "Yeah, I'll have the lunch special. Let's do fettuccini alfredo with a side of garlic toast and a Caesar salad."

Stella scribbled madly away in her notebook and nodded. "And, for you, Mrs. Owens?" Always so polite.

"I'll just have the chicken noodle soup. I'm not very hungry," Jennifer said with sad eyes.

Penny's stomach churned yet again. How could she have let the affair go on for so long? She was a homewrecker, and the damage sat right in front of her, less than a foot away. She hated herself at that moment, for being the reason to cause another so much pain. She'd own up to it. She'd confess everything and beg for forgiveness. Her mother didn't raise her to be this kind of person, the kind who ruined another's life.

Stella nodded and strode to the kitchen, ripping the sheet off and handing the order to the cook on duty. The Cookery's door swung open and a few more Crimsonians bopped inside. Stella greeted them, and her twang echoed throughout the wide-open room.

"What was I saying?" Jennifer asked.

"You were asking about Jayson," Penny croaked.

Jennifer nodded with recognition and took another deep breath. "That's right. Sorry, pregnancy brain," she said with a shrug. "So, I think something is going on with him. Have you noticed anything different?"

Penny's pulse quickened and she could have sworn she heard her own heartbeat. "Like what? Different how?"

"He's been acting differently for the past few days. Well, he's been weird for a little while now, you know, distant, but in the past few days, it's gotten worse. He's gone all hours of the day, smells like cigarette smoke, and he gets all sketched out if I ask any questions."

Jennifer's eyes bore into Penny's with fierce desperation for the truth. Any bit of information. She needed answers, and she needed them now.

"Hmmm," Penny said, biting her lip. After a few moments, she tasted blood swimming inside her mouth, washing over her tongue. She took a sip of water and drank until the glass was nearly empty.

"We got into a huge fight on Sunday, actually," Jennifer said.

Penny furrowed her brow. She wondered when they could have fought. Jayson had stayed late to cover for her during layout while she went to investigate Harper's disappearance. Did something happen when he got home?

"I actually got really upset about that little girl going missing," Jennifer admitted and pointed to her stomach. "Hormones, ya know?"

"Well, I don't actually know, but I can imagine," Penny replied. "So, he started acting weird when you brought up Harper Golden?"

Jennifer nodded emphatically. "I just don't know, Penny. I'm worried. I think he might be seeing someone else, too."

Penny choked on the sip of water she'd just taken and

suffered a coughing fit of epic proportions. Stella rushed over and patted her back.

"Lordy, Lord! Are you okay, Miss Penny?"

"I'm. Fine," Penny squeaked. Jennifer moved to stand, but Penny waved her away. "I'm okay, really!" The last thing she needed was Jennifer to comfort *her*.

Stella stepped away from the table and returned a few moments later with a tray carrying their lunches. Steam poured from Jennifer's soup and Penny's pasta. If only she didn't feel nauseated and weak in the knees, she might be able to actually enjoy the food before her.

"Let me know if y'all need anything else, ya hear?" Stella asked.

"Thank you," Penny and Jennifer said in unison.

Jennifer's head dropped toward the table as she absent-mindedly stirred her soup. Her shoulders slumped and her entire body slouched while one hand still massaged her protruding belly which sat against the edge of the table.

"I think he may be regretting the decision to have kids," Jennifer whispered.

Penny racked her mind for any recollections to support Jennifer's theory. Jayson had been acting strangely this week, but why? It couldn't have been guilt about their affair, considering it'd been going on for some time now and he hadn't previously shown any remorse. The only other notable event to have happened was Harper's disappearance. But why would it so negatively impact him to the point of starting fights with his wife and acting distant? Did he know something he wasn't telling anyone else?

"I'm sorry, Jennifer. I'm honestly not sure," Penny said, only half lying.

Jennifer nodded and only took a few tastes of her soup before asking Stella for a to-go container. Penny barely touched her lunch, either, but knew it'd last well enough for dinner if she could stomach it.

Something was going on with Jayson; now it was a fact, not just her imagination playing tricks on her. Penny had picked up on it, and now Jayson's wife had, too. What was he hiding and what did it have to do with Harper Golden?

CHAPTER ELEVEN

WEDNESDAY, OCTOBER 9, 2019

P enny left Crimson's Cookery with more food in her carry-out box than in her belly. A sour taste which had nothing to do with lunch lingered in her mouth. Penny promised herself to take Jayson aside as soon as possible and break things off with him. Whatever was going on with him, it was affecting his marriage, his wife, and she didn't want a part in it any longer.

For the longest time, she hadn't cared who she hurt with the affair, but after seeing the pain ebb and flow within Jennifer's eyes, she couldn't bear to know she was the one who caused her turmoil. Just because she didn't care about having a healthy relationship didn't mean she could partake in ruining another's. Jayson would have to accept it, too. She wouldn't let him talk her into continuing their tryst. It was over, and it would never happen again.

Penny leaned against the *Chronicle*'s office, in the alleyway next to the Cookery. The cold surface sank through her jacket and chilled her skin. The wind whipped in every which direction and the few autumn leaves left swirled in the street as though an invisible blender mixed them about.

Out of the corner of her eye, Penny noticed a disheveled woman milling about, posting signs on every telephone pole on Main Street. The woman donned stained sweatpants and wore a messy bun atop of her head. Penny turned her head to see the woman better and realized exactly who it was: Harper's mother. Upon further investigation, she also noticed the signs Sandy posted were missing ads for her daughter. The sheets of paper whipped in her hands, threatening to be swept away in the whistling wind.

Penny pushed off the side of the building and slowly approached Sandy in the same manner someone would greet a wounded animal.

"Mrs. Golden?"

Sandy looked up, her bloodshot eyes contrasting terribly against her pale skin. "Oh, hi," she said wiping her nose with her sleeve.

Penny carefully reached to touch Sandy's forearm. "I know words won't mean much now, but I hope Harper will come home safely. Is there anything I can do for you?"

Sandy sneered. "What, you want to write another article? Your friend has already been pestering me wanting more details."

"My friend?"

"Yeah, that other reporter," Sandy said venomously. "Keeps calling my house."

"I'm sorry, Mrs. Golden. No one at the *Chronicle* is writing another article on you or your daughter. In fact, we've been strictly told not to. Did the reporter give you his name?"

Sandy turned away and stapled another poster to the pole. Little Harper smiled in the picture, sending chills down Penny's spine. Where was Harper now? Was she still alive? Who would take her? And why?

"Jayson, he said his name was," Sandy said. "My husband and I have already told him we have nothing more to say."

"I'm truly sorry, and I will talk to him right away. He won't bother you anymore," Penny promised.

Sandy looked up and peered into Penny's eyes. A single tear squeezed out and slid down her face. "I'm scared," she whispered.

Penny nodded and stepped a smidge closer to the mourning mother. "We just have to keep our hope alive that she'll come home soon."

Sandy frowned. "Hope and faith aren't going to bring my little girl home."

Penny sighed. Entirely abandoning her typical character, she pulled Sandy into her arms and held her tightly. She felt her stiffen against her touch but slowly relaxed into the embrace. Sandy's body quivered, and sobs erupted from deep within her throat. They held each other like that for what felt like an eternity before Sandy pulled away.

"Thank you. For your kindness," she said. "I'm sorry I was so rude to you. I know you were just trying to do your job."

Penny waved her away. "You have nothing to apologize for, Mrs. Golden."

"Please, call me Sandy. Will you be coming to the vigil tomorrow? We're having one at the high school," she said.

Penny nodded. "I'd love to."

"Maybe you could write a small article about it?" Sandy let a weak smile escape her chapped lips.

A jolt of excitement surged through Penny. That would be an excellent opportunity for her and the paper. And, since Sandy provided her permission, Peter, in theory, shouldn't have a problem with it. But the nagging feeling of curiosity scratched at Penny's brain: Why was Jayson pestering the Goldens about Harper's disappearance? He knew they were basically off limits. Instances of his continued peculiar behavior piqued Penny's suspicions. What was going on with him?

"I'd love to," Penny said.

An awkward silence emerged between the two women and Sandy looked down at the bleached sidewalk and shuffled her feet. "Well, then. I'll see you tomorrow. I'm going to finish putting up these signs."

"Sounds good, Sandy. I will be there tomorrow. Please let me know if there's anything else I can do for you and your family."

With that, Penny waved weakly and left Sandy to finish stapling the flyer to the telephone pole. She looked one last time over her shoulder at the solemn woman, and her heart ached. She doubted her daughter would survive her abduction. Too much time had already passed.

Penny walked into the *Crimson Chronicle* office to see Jayson typing madly away at his computer. He didn't even flinch when she sat down beside him.

"What?" he asked, his eyes focused on the keyboard as the sounds of his fingers tapping the keys filled the empty room.

"Why have you been calling Sandy Golden?" Penny asked.

That was cause enough for Jayson to stop what he was doing. He slowly turned his head. Jayson's eyes appeared nearly as bloodshot as Sandy's. Penny jumped and slid her chair back a few inches.

"Whoa. What's wrong with you?"

"Nothing. And how did you hear that I was calling her?" He narrowed his eyes.

"She told me," Penny said, trailing off. "Why are you bothering her? You know Peter said we had to back off."

"You shouldn't get involved in people's business," Jayson said with lowered eyes.

"Dude? What is up with you lately?" Penny asked, taken aback.

"Nothing."

Penny wrinkled her nose and looked around the office. The distinct scent of body odor and onions lingered in the air. "What's that smell?"

Jayson returned his gaze to his computer screen, where he'd begun the draft article for the talent show. Penny carefully watched the man next to her. Jayson had first told her he loved her behind the bleachers after homecoming. She couldn't believe her ears when he'd said it and couldn't believe that she'd said it back. Once she'd returned the favor, he'd smashed his lips against hers in a drunken stupor.

Penny pressed her fingers to her lips, almost as if she could remember Jayson's touch from all those years ago. But, as with life and love, not everything was meant to last. So many of their friends had thought they'd make it; they'd cross the finish line together old and gray. But they didn't. Except, a handful of years later, they'd found each other again, even though Jayson was already claimed. Now, Penny knew deep in her heart; it was time to end it again.

"Jayson, can we talk?"

Without looking up, he said, "About what?"

Penny glanced around the office; no one else was there. Not even Peter.

"About us?"

This caught Jayson's attention, and he turned to face her. "What about us?"

Again, Penny glanced around despite the office's lack of noise and the absence of everyone else. "Maybe we can go somewhere else?"

Jayson scoffed. "No one is here. Just say it. I already know what you're going to say, anyway."

"You do?" Penny chewed the inside of her cheek until she tasted the metallic, warm liquid.

"Yeah, but go ahead," Jayson said and rolled his eyes.

Penny rarely saw this side of Jayson. The fun-loving man who always found the silver lining had vanished. Something was going on with him, but she didn't know what.

"I think we have to stop seeing each other. You know, romantically."

Jayson snorted. "Fine."

Penny stood from the chair and paced around the office. The wind whipped outside and even darker clouds loomed in the distance.

"Fine? That's all you have to say?"

Jayson turned in his seat to face her, his back to the computer. "What do you want me to say, Penny? You want me to beg you to stay with me?"

"Well, no," she said and paused. "It just seems like you don't care either way."

Jayson put his head in his hands and talked through his fingers. "It's over, okay? I get it. Just business from now on."

Penny hadn't expected this reaction. She thought Jayson *would* beg, or at least, not give up so easily. She knew he loved his wife, but if history had proven anything, he also still loved her. And she never really knew, inside her heart, if she actually loved him back. Sometimes, we chose what was safe, what was easy, and hold on that for as long as we could.

"Okay, well, thanks for understanding," Penny said slowly.

Jayson spun back to face his computer and grunted. Penny, on the other hand, couldn't explain the pulsing pit in her stomach and why she felt like something was terribly wrong. Would she figure it out in time? Or would life surprise her yet again?

CHAPTER TWELVE

THURSDAY, OCTOBER 10, 2019

O minous clouds rolled in for most of the afternoon, blocking out the sun from the sky. Scattered showers pelted Crimson Falls on and off all day, too. Despite the less-than-ideal forecast, though, the Goldens wouldn't put off their plans for a nighttime vigil for their missing girl. Harper still hadn't been found, nor had there been any new leads. Pressure mounted on the police department for some kind of answer, for an explanation, but none came. It was almost as if Harper had vanished into thin air. Gone without a trace.

"Are you sure you don't mind staying a little longer?" Penny asked her mother's nurse.

"Not at all, dear. Please send my prayers and well wishes when you go," she said.

Penny nodded, kissed her mother's forehead, and headed out of the house. She sported houndstooth rain boots, a black hoodie, and a jean jacket over the top. Raindrops stung her forehead as she sprinted from the front door to her car. She drove in silence toward the high school where the Goldens planned to have the vigil.

Before she'd left home, Penny charged her phone to one hundred percent. Since Sandy said she could cover the event, she wanted to make sure her phone had as much juice as possible. She still hadn't broached the subject with Peter, but again, she thought if the Goldens approved it, Peter wouldn't have any excuse *not* to print it in the next edition.

Penny's jaw dropped as she pulled into the school's parking lot and noticed almost every space was filled.

Holy cow, she thought.

She had no idea what to expect and how many people would turn up to support the Goldens. Turned out, the entire city wanted to lend their thoughts and prayers.

Penny circled the lot several times and finally parked on the grass beside the dumpster. It wasn't technically a spot, but every other one was taken. She grabbed for her umbrella on the passenger seat and headed outside into the slow but steady showers of the evening.

She strode across the lot toward the front doors of the school where hundreds and hundreds of Crimsonians stood, some with umbrellas, and others soaked to the bone. With one hand holding the umbrella, she reached her other hand into her pocket and pulled out her phone. She opened her camera app and snapped a few photos of the scene. She took some landscapes and some portraits. Once satisfied with her shots, Penny stepped over a few puddles and joined the mass of people huddled around the Goldens as they stood on a slightly raised platform. Sandy's eyes hadn't lost the red tint. Mr. Golden stared straight ahead with no emotion whatsoever. He looked frozen in time, immobile, vacant.

Behind them, an easel held an almost life-sized picture of Harper on the swings, her red hair glowing in the twilight of what appeared to be a summer evening. A few of the news crews from nearby cities recorded the grieving parents as they held each other's hands. Penny snapped a few more photos and turned to see which of the townspeople around her would provide her with a usable quote or two for her story.

One of her mother's friends, Wendy, wept on her husband's shoulder, both under an umbrella. Penny excused herself and maneuvered toward Wendy with her phone in her hand, ready to push *record*.

"Hi, Wendy," Penny said.

Wendy turned her head and revealed streams of mascara dribbling down her cheeks, which were overly done with a rosy blush.

"Penny, so good to see you. How's your mother?"

"The same," Penny replied with a fake smile. It was easier to fabricate positivity than to admit her mother's health grew slightly worse with each passing day.

"Please tell her I said hello."

Penny sensed the electricity in the air and thought the Goldens would begin the vigil at any moment. She needed a quote from Wendy before it started, and she didn't want to miss anything Sandy or her bereaved husband would say to all those in attendance.

"Wendy, would you mind if I got a quote from you about Harper's disappearance?"

Wendy's eyes, immersed in blue eyeshadow, expanded and a slight smile crossed her lips. "Oh! For the paper?"

Penny nodded. "Yes, ma'am."

Wendy cleared her throat, which was Penny's cue to press *record*.

The rain overhead slowed down to a misting, but thunder rumbled in the near distance. The storm wasn't over yet, in fact, it may have just begun.

"It's a terrible ordeal!" Wendy exclaimed.

Her husband nodded emphatically. "Terrible!"

"We hope poor Harper comes home soon and whoever

had a hand in her disappearance is brought to a swift and fair justice!"

Penny smiled and gave the thumbs up. It was a generic quote, but it'd have to do. Although, what else was there to say, really, about a missing girl? Everyone hoped she'd come home safely and the man, or woman, who took her was severely punished.

Mr. Golden tapped on the microphone while Sandy quickly blew her nose. Despite the rain, one could still see the tears streaming down the woman's face. Penny wondered how she held herself together, how she could come out in public during all of this.

"Thank you, everyone," Mr. Golden said.

Penny hit *record* again, hoping her phone would pick up the audio as best it could. She would need a decent sound file to transcribe it for her story later.

"We appreciate you all coming out tonight to support our family as we, again, plead for the safe return of our daughter, Harper Golden."

With a piercing stare, Mr. Golden looked straight into the news camera before him. "We ask that whoever took our daughter bring her home unharmed. We love her so very much, and all we want is to hold her again in our arms."

Beside Penny, Wendy pulled out a handkerchief and wept into the red cloth. Her husband rubbed her back, and it didn't take long for the other women in the vicinity to be reduced to shaking sobs, too.

"Harper is the light of our lives and the best thing that ever happened to us. Please bring her home!"

Then Sandy reached for the microphone and pulled it toward her quivering lips. "We will provide a thirty-thousand-dollar reward for anyone who can provide any information which leads to the recovery of our daughter. Please! We want our baby girl back!"

As if Mother Nature knew what was to happen next, the misting drops falling from the gray clouds stopped. It was as if the heavens wanted the vigil to carry on without any more gloom and sadness. Sandy's sister, who'd flown in from California, brushed aside her strawberry-blonde hair, the same as Harper's. She carried an oversized fabric tote on her shoulder and handed out single candlesticks, urging those in attendance to pass them along to their neighbors. Soon enough, every person in the audience held a white candle. Many people pulled out their lighters and ignited their sticks. They kissed their flames to the virgin wicks all around them until, now, not everyone just held a candle, but a lit one, too.

Artfully, Penny snapped a photo of her own lit candle using the Portrait mode on her iPhone. It would make an excellent addition to the story. Maybe she'd convince Peter to let her publish it above the fold again. Subtle orchestra music crooned from the few speakers set around the scene, and everyone linked arms, candles in hand.

Penny's breath caught in her throat while she absorbed it all. Even though Crimson Falls carried unimaginably bad luck within its borders, it never stopped the townspeople from coming together in moments of despair.

Out of the corner of her eye, Penny noticed Jayson and Peter storming away from the vigil. They strode across the parking lot toward the dumpster, exactly where Penny parked her car. A pang in her gut told her to follow them, and Penny usually tried to listen to her instincts. They were there for a reason, after all. Confident that she'd collected enough information, quotes, and photos for her story, Penny politely excused herself from the crowd and left the vigil behind. She extinguished her candle and tossed it in a nearby trash bin. Then, she opened up her umbrella for cover once more. The pitter-patter of her ex-lover's and boss's steps reverberated within the lot. She peeked from underneath her umbrella to see where they'd gone. It didn't take long for Penny to notice the two men hid behind the dumpster. The only indication of their presence was in the form of their rising voices, piercing her ears.

"I don't know what you think you saw, but you're dead wrong," one of them said.

"I saw what I saw!" the other quipped back, anger in his voice.

"You better watch yourself. Maybe you're just trying to cover for yourself, huh? Maybe *you're* the one hiding something!"

Penny's stomach sank. What the hell was going on? Who was hiding what? She quickly pulled out her phone and snapped a few more pictures, only this time, they weren't of people mourning, but of those arguing instead.

CHAPTER THIRTEEN

THURSDAY, OCTOBER 10, 2019

A vague sense of hope pulsed inside Harper's heart. The man holding her hostage seemed to believe she was Heather, whoever that may be, and Harper played perfectly into that mindset. While he still kept her in the basement, he removed the handcuffs from her wrists. She wasn't shackled to the cold, damp basement wall anymore.

He brought her more food during mealtimes and even a few snacks here and there. Her strength increased, as did her determination to escape. She needed a plan, though. One that wouldn't fail. The trust she'd worked to build with the man would be tarnished entirely if he caught her trying to escape. Hell, he might even hurt her as punishment.

Nothing in her young life thus far prepared her for such a challenge. English? Nope. Math? No. History? Nada.

But she used all of her energy to think long and hard about what she could do to leave the confines of her concrete cage. She needed a way to get upstairs. Once she made it to a better part of the house, she could further assess her situation and formulate a way to get out. Harper hoped with all of her heart she wasn't too far away from Crimson Falls. She had absolutely no idea where she was now. For all she knew, she could be next door to her own house. The man had blindfolded her after taking her from the park. He'd driven her around for an incredible amount of time. Taking turns and driving for long stretches. She hadn't kept up with where he'd taken her and which route he'd chosen.

It didn't matter, though. If they were still in the heart of Crimson Falls, it wouldn't be too difficult to find help. If they were outside her hometown, she'd run and run until she found help. Images of her mom and dad burned in her brain. One way or another, she'd find her way home. That was a promise she made to herself and wouldn't break it for anything.

Thunder rumbled outside, and Harper pulled her knees to her chest. For hours and hours, she thought of a way to convince the man to bring her upstairs. Finally, she had an idea. She hoped it would work. It *had* to work.

Upstairs, the thumps of footsteps shook the floor. The doorknob of the basement door creaked as it turned. The man hobbled down the steps. The faint glow from the lights upstairs barely illuminated the basement, but it was just enough for Harper to see her own hands.

"Heather, baby. How is daddy's little girl doing?"

Bile rose in Harper's throat, but she forced it back down.

"Daddy?" she whined.

"Yes, baby?"

Fried chicken permeated the air as did the faint smell of stale beer. Harper's stomach turned, and she took a deep breath, hoping to steady herself, to focus.

"Something's happened. I need your help."

The man sat beside Harper and pulled her into his lap. Goosebumps shimmied down Harper's arm. The man's touch brought the bile back up into her throat.

"What is it? Tell Daddy what's wrong," he said soothingly.

"I think I got my womanhood," Harper said and held her breath.

In health class, their teacher, Mrs. Banes, taught the boys and girls about what would happen when they reached puberty. The boys and girls were divided separately so they could learn about the changes in their own bodies without the giggles from the others. Harper remembered panicking and sheer fright enveloping her body when Mrs. Banes told the girls that soon, they would get their periods and once a month they would need to use sanitary napkins. Harper hoped it would never happen to her. How gross! And yet it seemed like the perfect way for the man to let her upstairs. He wouldn't let her sit down in the basement in her own filth, would he?

Silence filled the air. Harper's heart drummed against her chest. Would it work? Would he believe her? Would he help her?

"Hmmm," he said. "Are you sure?"

Harper's teeth bit into her lip. "Yes, Daddy. My tummy hurts so much, and I felt the blood."

More silence.

"Well," the man said after what felt like an eternity, "We can't have that, can we? My little baby Heather is a woman!"

Harper exhaled.

"I guess we should get you upstairs and get you cleaned up, huh?"

Harper nodded emphatically. "Please!"

"I'll have to run to the store and get you some supplies, though," he said slowly.

The man pulled something out of his pocket and while Harper sat in his lap, he wrapped the object around her eyes: it was his handkerchief.

"You've got to promise me, though, Heather. Promise me you won't run away from Daddy."

Exhilaration whipped through Harper's body. Hope tasted that much closer. Freedom was that much closer. "Yes, Daddy. Of course. I want to stay with you forever!"

She added the last part because it always worked when she feigned sick to stay at home with her parents. As soon as she whipped out that phrase, her parents melted into the palms of her hands.

The man pulled her closer to his chest and squeezed her body like a python. "I love you so much, Heather. Let's get you all cleaned up."

He gently pushed Harper off his lap and pulled her into a standing position with him. The man heaved her over his shoulder and with some difficulty, they walked up the basement steps. Harper's pulse raced with every step toward the soft light at the top of the staircase. Each stair represented a step closer to freedom, a step closer to seeing her real dad and her mom.

With the handkerchief shielding her eyes, Harper couldn't make out anything specific once they reached the landing and the man closed the basement door behind them, but she could sense so much more. She smelled the faint aroma of a microwavable dinner; she heard the gentle clicking of a manual clock, she felt the cold air brushing against her skin. The man cleared his throat and brought her into a new room, one that seemed more clinical, deodorized. He set her down, and she felt cool porcelain against her skin. Vanilla and cinnamon tickled her nose. The man turned on the faucet and rinsed his hands in the sink, at least that's what she thought he was doing.

"You wash up, okay? I'm going to run to the store and get you what you need."

"Thanks, Daddy," Harper replied as sweet as pie.

The man kissed her forehead and Harper didn't even flinch. She didn't feel revulsion sizzling under her skin. All she could think about was the taste of freedom lingering on her chapped lips. Soon, she'd be out of this house and back in her own.

The man closed the door behind him, and Harper heard a faint clicking noise as he did so. Her heart sank a touch. Did he lock her inside? She waited until the roar of a car engine sounded and then faded away. The man was gone.

She ripped off her blindfold and dropped it onto the black and white tiled floor. Harper lunged for the bathroom door to find it was locked from the outside. She shook the handle vigorously to no avail. He'd locked her inside. Tears of desperation flooded Harper's vision as the notion of freedom seemed to slip through her fingertips like water. How would she escape this house now? How would she get away?

She whipped around to see a window on the other side of the room. She leaped toward it and pushed it up, trying to force the wood to move upward. It wouldn't budge. She'd lost almost all her strength and energy in captivity.

Harper knew she wasn't any closer to escaping and soon enough when the man returned, she'd most likely be forced back into the basement and back into the darkness of captivity.

CHAPTER FOURTEEN

THURSDAY, OCTOBER 10, 2019

P enny couldn't shake the dread rattling in her bones after witnessing Jayson and Peter's dispute behind the dumpsters. She had to know more; she needed to find out what was going on. Despite her and Jayson's recent awkwardness and distance, they'd always been close enough friends to tell each other secrets, pass along pertinent information, and just generally keep in touch about everything and anything. But he hadn't told her what had been keeping him on the edge of his seat this past week. All of his unease seemed to stem from Harper's disappearance, and now, after seeing the two men quip in the parking lot of the vigil, she was sure it *had* to do with the little girl.

Even Peter had kept his distance from her this week. Why were the men in her life steering clear of her? Was it because they had something to hide and they knew, without a doubt, she'd uncover it?

Penny hid in her car until she was sure Jayson and Peter left the high school parking lot. Her instincts told her she needed to figure out what was happening in Crimson Falls.

What if she ignored her gut feeling and Harper ended up hurt, or worse, dead?

Without a second thought, Penny turned the key in her ignition and sped out of the lot. The vigil wound down. Most people swarmed the parking lot to their cars, too. She cruised through Crimson Falls toward Peter's house. She figured the best way to get to the truth was to face it head-on.

Peter was like a second father to her; surely he'd explain what she just saw. And, if Jayson were guilty of something, maybe they could go to the police together. Would it hurt like hell to turn in Jayson into the authorities? Of course, it would, but if he had anything to do with Harper's kidnapping, then he wasn't the man she thought he was in the first place.

Penny drove up the winding driveway to Peter's dated three-story Victorian. Only a few lights were on, including the downstairs living room and just one light upstairs on the second floor. But his car wasn't in the driveway.

She parked on the grassy lot underneath a swaying willow tree and pulled her keys out of the ignition. Penny sat there, her breathing labored and uneven.

I could at least knock. Couldn't hurt, right? she thought.

She opened the car door and her boots sank into the mushy turf of the yard. The sky rained down more drizzles, but she didn't want to fuss with her umbrella. She already looked like a wet dog, why worry about it now?

Penny hiked across the stone driveway and more messy mud. Several pieces of garbage littered the yard and she could see his dumpster can's lid had flown open from the wind. She stepped over a few empty beer bottles before she reached the front door.

Blood pulsed through her veins and her head spun with anticipation. Why was she so nervous? It was Peter. Peter!

The man who practically raised her outside of her own home. Surely, he'd tell her what was going on to put her nerves at ease.

Penny knocked on the door and held her breath.

Nothing.

She knocked again.

Not a sound.

She knocked furiously one last time and waited, her teeth nibbling on her cheek once more. But, nothing happened. No one came to the door, and no one made a sound. Finally giving up, Penny ambled back to her car as the wind whipped her hair every which way. The dumpster lid smacked against the side of the house in a foreboding fashion.

As the storm swirled around her, Penny swore she heard something else. She looked over her shoulder, but no one was there. Shivers shimmied down her spine. Penny crossed her arms over her middle. Her breathing intensified as her heart rate increased exponentially.

She looked over her other shoulder, but again, she saw and heard nothing. In the distance, she swore she heard someone's voice. A yelp, even. But no one was there.

Penny looked down at her phone and noticed the time. She was a half hour later than she'd promised the nurse.

Shit!

Penny drove away from Peter's house back to her own but couldn't look away from the Victorian in her rear-view mirror.

CHAPTER FIFTEEN

FRIDAY, OCTOBER 11, 2019

Early on Friday morning, Penny's alarm shook her out of her uneven sleep before the sun kissed the horizon. She didn't have to be at work for another few hours, but she wanted to sneak into the office early to work on her piece about Harper's vigil before anyone else started their shifts for the day.

She pulled herself out of bed and peeled her damp t-shirt over her head. Most of her hair, damp, too, was matted and tangled. Visions of children crying for their parents and scratching against concrete walls filled her nightmares throughout the night. Even if she woke up, tossed and turned, and fell back asleep, the dreams only resumed where they'd left off. A handful of times, her own distressed yelps roused her from the persistent nightmares.

After immersing herself in a brief, yet relaxing, steaming hot shower, Penny tiptoed to the kitchen and dug through the pantry until she found an older Cheerio box. Inside, a secret stash of bills lay folded for emergency use only.

She needed a little extra money to pay Sophie's overtime

for the additional hours she'd taken care of her mother this week. And, Lord knew, her reporter's salary wouldn't cover much more than the basics. Penny pulled out a few extra Andrew Jacksons, stuffed them in the back pocket of her faded black jeans, and deposited the cereal box back into the depths of the pantry. Her mother told her never to be too careful with her savings and Penny took that to heart. Before they hired Sophie, one of the nurses from the agency stole a few dollars here and there from the kitchen drawer. Penny had to borrow a little from Peter to pay their water bill that month. Needless to say, Penny fired that nurse on the spot. It wasn't her finest moment, but Peter had taken care of her, as he always did.

At the thought of him, guilt snaked through her body as she set out the door for the newspaper office. She knew the Golden case was technically still off limits, but Peter would have to let it go to print once he read the piece and saw the accompanying pictures. Even a stubborn man like him couldn't deny a fine example of journalism. She figured he was still tormented by his daughter's death and Harper's disappearance only reminded him of that, but he shouldn't let that get in the way of reporting on an important story.

A mixture of sleet and snow fell from the dark sky. Shivers ran up and down Penny's arm despite her wearing a hoodie and a coat. Barely any other cars shared with the road with Penny as she cruised toward the office. She couldn't help but notice the paper signs with Harper's sweet face hung limply from the posts along Main Street, the rain making them soggy like Shredded Wheat that sat too long.

Would she ever find her way home? And if the worst were to happen, and she didn't, would the town forget about her as they did the missing girls from the past? Would the girl with the crooked teeth and strawberry-blonde hair become just a memory? A faded dream from many moons ago? Her parents wouldn't soon forget the gaping hole in their hearts, but could the rest of Crimson Falls keep her in their thoughts, too? Or, would the idea of Harper Golden disappear like a wisp of smoke?

Penny parked her car and sprinted toward the back door to the *Chronicle*'s office. Only a select few knew the security code to the building, and she was one of them. Jayson was another, but only because he'd weaseled it out of her a couple of years ago. Jayson had procrastinated writing a few of his upcoming articles, and as fate would have it, an insane storm had passed through town, and almost everyone's power had gone out. Penny hadn't been able to leave her mother: it had been one of her bad days. But the *Chronicle* had a generator, and Jayson had promised to take over layout for the next month if she gave him the code so he could finish his assignments. She'd obliged and enjoyed having the next four Sundays off instead of working on layout night.

Penny eased out of her leather coat and whipped it around, attempting fruitlessly to dry it off. She hung it up on the coat rack by the door and rubbed her hands together. Stalking across the carpet, Penny made her way into the breakroom and started a pot of coffee. She could use the whole damn pot considering how sleep had eluded her last night. As the steaming coffee trickled from the machine, Penny closed her eyes and leaned against the wall.

Silence.

So many people took it for granted. They didn't take the time to appreciate the absence of chaos. But not Penny. She pined for it. No one badgering her, no one asking to take them to the bathroom, or to make sure she chose the best quote for her story. No one to interfere. No one to impress upon her.

Once the pot was filled to the brim, she poured herself

some into her mug that read, *I Like it Inverted Pyramid Style*, a white Elephant gift she'd received at the last office Christmas party.

Penny poured powder creamer into her coffee and about three too many sugar packets. She set the mug down on her desk, and a few drops spilled onto her keyboard. Her computer hummed as it booted up and Penny nibbled her cuticles while she waited.

She sipped her coffee slowly at first, then once she adjusted to its temperature, she gulped it down. The desire for caffeine controlled her every thought. Out of nowhere, though, the memory of her and Jayson staying late on layout night with the help of coffee and Baileys sprung through Penny's consciousness. Her mouth watered for the taste of a little booze in her coffee. What could it hurt? No one else was here. And, it never affected her ability to write. In fact, sometimes, it helped.

Like a child in a candy store, Penny trotted back into the breakroom, opened the fridge, and peered behind all the soda for the little shots of Baileys they'd hidden. Except, she soon realized, they were all gone. Had they actually drank them all that Sunday night? She supposed they did. But Jayson almost always kept a bottle of booze in his drawer. For special occasions, or for the nasty ones. With a little less bounce in her step, Penny strolled back to the office area and dug out Jayson's desk key from his mug of pens and paper clips. She was the only one who knew it was there. She turned the small golden key into the keyhole for the top drawer, expecting to pull it open and see the bulge of the bottle under a few empty folders.

Except, she saw something else. Something she never expected to see, let alone discover in a drawer at the *Chronicle*.

There in front of her, clear as day, was a pair of muddy,

pink sneakers. The same exact sneakers Harper wore the day she disappeared. Penny dropped her mug of coffee and the porcelain shattered, spilling its steaming contents all over the floor.

CHAPTER SIXTEEN
FRIDAY, OCTOBER 11, 2019

P enny backed away from the drawer as if a hissing viper lay in it, ready to pounce. Her heart throbbed against her chest and threatened to explode. Her breath caught in her throat and she forgot to exhale.

Why would a pair of little girl's sneakers be in his desk drawer at work? A pair of sneakers which matched the description of Harper's to a T? There had to be a logical explanation, right? A valid reason? But what would that even be? What excuse would Jayson have to explain it? Penny collapsed into her chair as dizziness grasped at her consciousness and tugged at her ability to think clearly.

What would she do now? What *could* she do now?

I should call him and ask him point-blank, she thought. *But, no. What if he lashes out? What if he did take her and he hurts her?*

Flashes of their relationship through the years flashed before her eyes. The hours they'd spent together, working, playing, getting in trouble, and so much more. She'd never thought he could be capable of such a vile crime. He simply wasn't the type. Sure, he wasn't the best husband, not by a mile, but did that automatically mean he'd hurt a child? And, if it *was* him, how would that explain all the missing girls in years past? Sadness enveloped her. She couldn't breathe. She couldn't think. This man loved her. Was a man capable of love also capable of murder? Could those two traits co-exist within a person?

It didn't make a lick of sense — not one bit.

Penny raised her hand and held it at eye level; it shook violently. She wiped her hands on her jeans and gripped the denim. She desperately tried to steady herself. To think clearly. To figure out what to do next.

Who could she call? Talk to? Vent to? Before she had time to ponder the answer to that question, the back door opened and the familiar sound of the alarm being disarmed chimed within the silence. Penny gulped and slammed Jayson's drawer closed. Beads of sweat trickled down the back of her neck. She tapped her foot against the floor, ignoring the spilled coffee.

She squeezed her eyes shut and hoped it wasn't Jayson coming in early. She wasn't ready to face him. Not yet.

Behind her, someone cleared their throat.

Peter.

"Mornin', Penny. You're here early," he said.

Penny spun slowly in her desk chair and gulped. "Hey, boss. How's it going?"

He narrowed his eyes and craned his neck to see what was on her computer screen. "What are you working on? I figured you'd be penning your talent show article tomorrow, after the fact."

"Actually—" she said.

Peter watched her carefully, as though he waited for the other shoe to drop. Penny wanted to broach the subject of the vigil piece, but that only reminded of her Harper, who led to her think of the shoes in the drawer next to hers. Jayson. Harper. What the hell was going on in Crimson Falls?

"Can we talk?" Penny asked, clearing her own throat.

Peter eyed his favorite employee up and down. "Sure," he said slowly. "Everything okay?"

"Not particularly," Penny replied.

Peter walked past Penny and the spilled coffee and nodded toward his office. "Come on."

Penny stood on shaky legs and followed Peter into his office, stepping over the stained carpet which reeked of French vanilla artificial creamer. She couldn't calm herself down despite all of her best efforts.

Peter flicked on his light and illuminated the room, including himself. Penny noticed his bloodshot eyes and his distinct pallor. He looked like he'd seen a ghost, too. And, maybe he had. It wasn't uncommon this time of year for those in Crimson Falls to lose themselves, to morph into another person, to fall into dangerous habits.

"You okay?" Penny asked. She sat down across from Peter and waited for his reply.

"Just, you know, that time of year," he said and looked longingly toward the headshot of his late daughter.

"I totally get it," Penny said. A lump formed in her throat and she begged herself to open up to him. She needed guidance and someone to tell her how to handle the current situation. Tears lingered in the corners of her eyes, ready to fall down her cheeks.

"What's that you wanted to talk about?"

Penny cracked each and every one of her knuckles. Then she gripped the arms of her chair. "I think someone I know, we know, rather, has done something wrong."

A sheen of glittering sweat formed on Peter's forehead, and he pulled out a handkerchief to wipe it away.

"Go on," he said.

Penny stared at her feet like a little girl in the principal's office. She was about to tattle on one of her most dependable allies, one of her oldest friends. "I found something in Jayson's desk."

"Oh?" Peter asked.

Penny cleared her throat and looked up toward her boss. "I think I found Harper Golden's sneakers in his drawer."

Silence filled the air. The humming of the incandescent bulbs overhead buzzed like a hummingbird. Peter stared at Penny until a heavy frown crossed his face. He stroked his unkempt beard.

"Show me," he finally said.

Penny pulled herself up from the chair and strode back into the main office area with Peter at her heels. The back of her top, now damp with sweat, clung to her body. Carefully, she placed her fingertips on the drawer's metallic handle and pulled gently before jumping backward. The drawer creaked open and revealed the sneakers. Harper's sneakers.

"Well, this isn't good," Peter said.

"What should we do?" Penny asked desperately. Tears snaked down her face.

"There's only one thing we can do."

Penny clutched her stomach as nausea washed over her. "What's that?"

"We call the police."

CHAPTER SEVENTEEN

FRIDAY, OCTOBER 11, 2019

T he cold porcelain chilled Harper to her bones, which appeared more prevalent in the young girl's cheeks. The man continued to feed her, but only barely. She lay curled up in the bathroom with all the lights off. She liked it better this way when he wasn't here. When he didn't visit and speak to her in baby talk as though she were his child.

The night before, though, he wasn't happy with her and Harper suffered the consequences.

The strange man had returned to the house with her feminine products as promised. He'd knocked on the door with a polite rap and instructed her to put on her blindfold. He'd only come in if she did so.

"Cover your eyes, Heather. If you don't, Daddy will be mad," he said.

As requested, Harper put on the blindfold and sat on top of the toilet seat, her legs jittering against it. She held her breath and waited for him to enter. The door squeaked as a cold draft swept into the bathroom. She heard heavy foot-steps and the bathroom door close again. This time, however, she wasn't alone. The man breathed heavily as he tossed the bag of supplies at the girl's feet.

"There you go, sweetie," he said softly.

Harper sat on her hands, concealing something she didn't want the man to see. The entire time he was gone, she'd sharpened the edge of his toothbrush against the windowsill until she created a pointed edge. She saw it on a movie once and thought she could give it a go herself. Since the man wouldn't leave her alone in an unlocked room, she had to figure out a way around that. She needed a way to circumvent the man entirely. And what better way than for him to be taken out completely? She shivered on the toilet seat while she concealed her weapon. She wasn't sure she could pull it off. The most she'd ever hurt a person was during gym class when she'd accidentally hit Jimmy in the head playing dodgeball. Besides that? She'd never been in the business of causing pain. No matter how many kids teased her at school for various things like her red hair or her missing teeth.

She sensed the man kneel before her and could feel his warm, stale breath against her face. He grasped her cheeks in his hands and kissed her forehead.

"It's almost your special day," he said. "Tomorrow, we will celebrate."

"Okay," Harper replied meekly.

Visions of running to her mother and father rushed through her head, and she'd never wanted to be in their arms more in her entire life. She wanted the warmth of her mother's bosom against her and the roughness of her father's beard scratching her cheek. She took a deep breath, and in a flash, she hopped off the toilet and swung madly in the air with the toothbrush knife in her hand. She caught the man and felt the tip of the makeshift-blade graze against his skin. The stranger yelped and stumbled backward into the tub, ripping the shower curtain from its rings in the process.

"Heather! What the hell?" he cried.

Without time to remove her blindfold, Harper felt her way to the bathroom door and found its knob. She yanked on it, and the door jiggled free. She felt the freedom on the tip of her tongue. She was about to escape!

Harper took one step over the threshold of the bathroom. She reached for her blindfold, but then the man yanked at her hair. He pulled her back into the bathroom. Harper slammed against the cold tile. A ringing in her ears immediately pierced her senses like a siren. She couldn't be sure, but she thought she felt warm blood oozing from her head onto the floor.

"How could you, Heather?" the man shrieked with indignation. "I trusted you!"

Tears poured down Harper's cheeks and vomit collected in her throat. She turned over and heaved what little sustenance she had left in her belly. The contents of her stomach splattered against the floor and splashed back onto her cheeks and chin. She moaned in agony, and intoxicating sobs crippled her.

"I want my mommy and daddy!"

"I am your family!" the man cried. "Me! Only me!"

"No!" Harper shot back. "You're not my daddy! Take me home, you monster!"

She waited for the incoming blow, but it never came.

"I thought this time would be different, Heather," he said, seethingly. "But, it's got to happen like it always does."

Confusion seized her and Harper crawled backward until she felt the closed bathroom door against her shaking body.

"Get up!" the man ordered.

The venom in his voice convinced her not to mess with him. Harper used the door as leverage and shimmied upward until she stood, still wearing the blindfold. The stranger grabbed at her hair again and dragged her as he opened the bathroom door. The floor creaked under their weight. Harper felt chunks of her hair being ripped away with the man's grip on her. Fresh tears sprang from her eyes, and she cried out yet again for her parents.

Her captor led her down a flight of stairs, each step squeaking as they ventured downward. The man cleared his throat over and over again, muttering to himself about the past repeating itself.

"Please let me go! I won't tell anyone about you," Harper pleaded. But the man ignored her.

They reached the last step and subsequently the first floor. The man yanked at Harper and led her further until she heard the turning of a doorknob. A rush of cold air whipped against her body and whirled her tangled hair. Shivers crept across her whole body. She wasn't dressed properly to go outside and yet that was exactly where the man was taking her.

With the blindfold still securely in place, she couldn't see where they were going, but she knew it was nighttime. The chill in the air was all she needed for evidence of the time of day. Harper's ears pricked at the sound of rustling leaves all around them. The man pushed her along, her bare feet stumbling upon little stones on the ground. She hopped up and down after stubbing her toe on a, particularly sharp one.

"Ouch!" she squealed.

The man ignored her still.

After what felt like miles and miles, the man finally brought Harper to a halt. She could feel asphalt now and could only guess they were near a road. Harper rubbed her arms, hoping to warm herself up to no avail. Her body quivered with fear and the freezing air assaulted her with every passing moment.

"I'm so sorry it has to be like this, Heather," the man said.

"It doesn't have to be like anything. Please let me go,

mister. I miss my family." Harper sobbed and shuddered against the man. But her tears wouldn't free her just as praying to the heavens wouldn't bring her any closer to her parents.

"It's time," the man said.

"Time for what?" Harper cried with chattering teeth.

In the distance, the hum of a semi truck's engine rattled through the night. Harper thought this could be her chance. She could be saved!

She concentrated and focused on the sound of the approaching truck. Surely, they'd see her and help her. They couldn't just drive by, right? Harper could smell the truck's fumes. She flailed her arms and pulled against the man's grasp.

"Help me! Help me!" she called into the night.

She could see the light from the truck illuminate her blindfold.

And, then, everything went all black again.

CHAPTER EIGHTEEN

SATURDAY, OCTOBER 12, 2019

News of Jayson's arrest spread through Crimson Falls like wildfire. The phones rang off the hook at the *Chronicle* as neighboring reporters, some from Arbordale, called and asked for a quote. Jayson's wife sobbed on cable TV and promised the viewers it was a mistake, that her husband could never hurt a child. She rubbed her own pregnant belly as tears gushed down her mascara-streaked cheeks.

The entire *Chronicle* office watched the TV in the break-room as local police handcuffed Jayson and shoved him into the back of the police cruiser. Before they closed the door on him, he looked straight into the camera and cried, "I'm innocent! I never touched her!"

Penny wanted to believe him; she wanted it all to be a sick joke. But how could she ignore the sneakers in his drawer? The Goldens confirmed they were Harper's, without a doubt. Chief Chapman and Officer Truman personally visited the newspaper's office to take each of the staff's statements, taking extra time with Penny.

She explained coming to the office early to work on a

story and looking for an extra phone charger. Naturally, she lied about what she was actually looking for in Jayson's desk. Penny couldn't help but feel guilty for blowing Jayson in, but what if he'd taken Harper? What if he'd hurt her? She didn't want to believe it, but she couldn't avoid the truth of what she found in his desk. Guilt nagged at her, but so did depression. She thought she knew Jayson. They'd been in love once. He'd treated her well. He'd taken care of her.

She didn't want to believe he was capable of such a crime, but then how did the sneakers get in his drawer? It would certainly explain his mysterious behavior over the past week. Would the police find her now? Was Harper still alive?

If it were any other publication, the *Chronicle* would have been all over the story, but since one of their own was locked up, they wanted to avoid the publicity at all costs. Peter instructed everyone to avoid talking to the public about it. He would draft a press release and an official statement on behalf of the *Crimson Chronicle* later that day.

Penny's stomach churned with despair. Even though she found the sneakers in Jayson's drawer, her instincts told her it wasn't the whole story. The reporter in her wanted more information, more answers.

She snuck out the back of the *Chronicle*'s office and pulled her hood over her head. Sleet poured from the sky and wind whipped her in the face. Penny unlocked her car and dove inside. She turned the key in the ignition, then pulled away from her parking spot. Penny's car rocked as she drove down Main Street and toward the woods, cemetery, and the Crimson Motel toward the edge of town. They'd moved Jayson overnight from the police station's holding cell to the Arbordale Jail. She drove to the jail in silence as she worked through what she'd say to Jayson. Penny couldn't piece together the reality of the situation. She'd barely slept the night before, and the haze of her fatigue clouded her vision.

Several times along the drive she dozed off and only woke as her tires grazed the bumpy ridges on the shoulder of the road.

Finally, she reached the jail and parked in the desolate lot. Apparently, there weren't that many visitors on a Saturday. Although, she'd had enough foresight to call the jail ahead of time to see if they accepted visitors on Saturdays at all.

She had about two hours left before visiting time ended. Plenty of time to see Jayson and ask him what the hell was going on. Penny stepped out of her vehicle, avoiding her reflection in the car window.

She took long strides across the lot, avoiding puddles until she reached the visitor entrance on the side of the aged, brick building. Inside, the jail appeared sterile and vacant, except for the guard chatting up the secretary at the front desk. The guard, a man in his mid-thirties with a bald spot, whispered into the woman's ear, causing her cheeks to redden and a giggle to escape her plum-colored lips.

Both turned, though, once Penny walked inside and approached the front desk. The guard stood up straight and revealed a hefty beer gut which hung well below the waist of his pants.

"How can we help you, miss?" he asked with his nose turned upright.

Penny ignored the man and faced the secretary as she blew a bubble and popped it loudly. "I'm Penny. I just called about visiting one of the guys here."

The woman nodded knowingly and nodded toward the metal detector. "You gotta go through there, hun. And, no phones allowed."

Penny obliged and handed her cell to the secretary before stepping through the dated metal detector, supervised by the overweight guard.

"Who ya here to see?" he asked as he led her through the

locked doors and into a room mimicking a school cafeteria. Penny knew she wouldn't be going to the common visiting area where the inmates were separated by glass, and that they must communicate with phones because part of the jail was undergoing renovations. Each table in the temporary visiting area had rings drilled into the table, presumably for the inmates and their handcuffs.

"A friend," Penny replied simply.

"I'll need their name if you want to see them," he said and rolled his eyes.

"Right. Yeah. Jayson Owens."

The guard's eyes illuminated like a Christmas tree. "The kidnapper? Took his sister and then took little Harper. He won't last very long in here."

Penny swallowed hard and dug her fingernails into the palms of her hands. She sat down at a table closest to the window. The guard pulled out his black matte walkie-talkie and mumbled a code into the mouthpiece.

Penny nibbled on her cuticles while she waited for Jayson to come to the visiting area. She stared outside and watched the bare trees sway back and forth in the storm. Penny wondered if she'd ever see the sun again.

Not for a while. At least not until October is over, she thought.

A deafening alarm rang twice, and a door buzzed open. In walked Jayson, donning an orange jumpsuit and walking like an Antarctic penguin in his shackles. Penny's breath caught in her throat and her stomach clenched with shock.

Jayson's sunken-in eyes were bloodshot and heavy. She doubted he'd slept a wink last night, the same as she. Under his left eye were shades of purple and blue. The guard snickered as Jayson walked by and sat down.

He narrowed his eyes, and if looks could kill, Penny would have dropped dead right then and there. She stared at her chewed nail beds, unable to speak.

"Why are you here?" Jayson asked, seething.

"I wanted to talk to you," Penny replied weakly.

Jayson burst into a fit of dark laughter. He sounded villainous and repulsed by Penny's presence. "You want to talk to me now? Now, that I'm in jail, you care to hear about my side of the story? I know it was you who turned me in. Peter told me so."

Penny looked up. "Peter told you it was me who found the sneakers?"

"Oh, yeah. Didn't you know? He said I had you to blame for being here."

Penny furrowed her brow and scrunched her face. She'd trusted Peter like family when she came to him with her discovery. Why would he blow her in like that? She shook her head.

"Well, do you have an explanation for why the sneakers were in there in the first place?"

Jayson growled, a deep guttural cry from within his throat. "I'm being set up!"

Two guards reached for their nightsticks, but Penny waved them away. She returned her gaze to Jayson and reached for his handcuffed hands. Jayson flinched and pulled away.

"Talk to me, Jayson. Did you take her?" Penny asked, her voice barely audible above the twittering guards in the corner.

"Look at me, Penelope. Look into my eyes. You know me. You know I didn't do this. I didn't hurt my sister and I didn't take Harper."

Penny stared into Jayson's eyes as he'd asked. She tried to delve deep into his soul as though his pupils were a window into his mind. Was he truly capable of taking Harper? Of hurting her? Of killing her? Even back then, she hadn't believed he had anything to do with Shannon's disappearance. She couldn't believe he was capable of hurting Harper, either. And yet, doubt nagged at her.

"If you didn't do it, then who did? Who put the sneakers in your desk?"

Jayson broke into a smile. "Don't you see? It's been in front of our faces all along."

"What, Jayson? What didn't we see?"

Penny broke the skin on her palms and blood oozed out of her gashes. She wiped them on her jeans, trying to conceal the wounds. Her pulse raced inside her chest.

"It's been him this whole time," he said.

"Who?"

Jayson leaned in as did Penny, until they were nearly nose to nose. "It's Peter."

CHAPTER NINETEEN

Penny stared at Jayson incredulously. "What did you just say?"

"You heard me. It's Peter. It's always been Peter," Jayson said, his voice low.

After a moment, Penny broke out into her own fit of laughter, catching the attention of the guards. They watched her intently, and one elbowed the other and spun his finger around as he pointed it to his own head.

"You gotta be shitting me, Jay. Are you fucking with me?"

Jayson remained stoic in his seat. "Think about it, Penny. All the girls, including Harper, who've gone missing have all disappeared around this time."

Penny finally calmed herself down but held her belly still. "That's because of the curse in Crimson Falls. You know that."

"Is it the curse that takes the girls or just encourages a sick bastard to do its bidding?"

She bit her lip and thought about Jayson's question. It was like the chicken or the egg conundrum. Who was truly responsible for the disappearances? *Someone* had to be blamed. There wasn't an invisible force snatching up the girls out of thin air.

"Why do you think that? What happened? Why would he do that?" She spat all her questions out at once.

Jayson brought his handcuffed hands to his face and buried his hands into them. He sighed heavily and hung his head.

"I saw him, Penny. I saw him take her that night," he said.

"Wait, what? You saw who?"

Her mind raced with the information presented to her. She pinched her leg discreetly, hoping to wake herself up from this awful nightmare. Peter wouldn't hurt a fly. He was practically a father to her. She would've known if he was capable of such a thing. She would have seen it coming!

Jayson craned his neck and saw the guards weren't paying them any attention at all.

"That night, when I went out for food before layout. I wanted to eat in my car before coming back to the office. I parked near the playground and saw Harper on her bike. She fell. Peter walked up to her. He talked to her for a few minutes, then carried her into his truck. They drove away together. I thought at first he was just giving her a ride home because it was so late. I picked up her sneakers to bring them to her later. Her parents helped us with our will, so I know where they live. But then the story broke about her disappearance."

Penny couldn't believe her ears. This couldn't be true. It couldn't be happening. She pinched herself again only to find she *was* firmly rooted in reality, not a dream world.

"Why didn't you go to the police right then and there?" she hissed.

"I had no proof. And I was scared," Jayson said, staring at his shackled feet.

"Well, now you have nothing to lose! Why don't you tell the police?"

Jayson looked up as a single teardrop plopped onto the table. "You know how it would go down, Penelope. It's an old boys' club. Peter is friends with almost all of the law enforcement. They'd never believe me. And now, with the shoes being found in my desk," he trailed off.

Tears sprang from Penny's eyes as she looked back at Jayson. "Why would he do it? Why would he hurt those girls? He was so kind to me growing up. You know how close we are. Why didn't he ever hurt me, if this is true?"

"I honestly don't know. You'll have to ask him," Jayson replied bitterly. "I would, but you know, I'm locked up for a crime I didn't commit."

"I saw you both arguing during the vigil. Behind the dumpsters," Penny said.

"You saw that?"

Just then, the wind ripped a weak branch off a tree outside the jail. It whipped and wound around in the air until it slammed against the glass window of the temporary visiting center. Penny and Jayson jumped in their seats. Penny squeaked and moved back in her chair. She took a few moments to gather herself.

"Yes, I did. What was that about?"

The lights flickered overhead, but Jayson continued. "I told him I saw him take her. And that I was going to expose him if he didn't take her home."

"What did he say?" Penny asked, on the edge of her seat.

"He denied it, of course. Said I must be projecting and that I was the one who really took her. He said if I didn't back off, he'd call the cops on me! Can you believe the prick?"

Penny nibbled on her cheek. "You think he planted the sneakers in your drawer?"

"I know he did. I had them in my trunk, and after our argument, they disappeared. He took them to plant them at my work station. Pretty fucking brilliant, if you ask me."

The lights flickered again and then went out completely. A siren sounded in the jail, and Penny covered her ears. "What is going on?"

The guards rushed over and grabbed Jayson under his arms and carried him away. The chubby guard from before burst into the visiting room and frantically ran toward Penny. "You've got to go, miss. The power's out. We have to secure the jail."

Penny didn't need to be told twice. She watched Jayson disappear behind another door. She jogged out of the jail and sprinted toward her car. More branches twirled in the air as if they were caught in a tornado. October thirteenth was coming. There was no avoiding it. You couldn't run, and you couldn't hide from the town's curse. She should go home and check on her mother. But there was someplace she needed to go first: Peter's house. Penny needed to find out the truth. Was Jayson playing her? Or was Peter truly the evil man of the legends of Crimson Falls, the monster who took little girls during October?

CHAPTER TWENTY

SATURDAY, OCTOBER 12, 2019

Penny pulled onto Peter's property and instantly remembered when she saw the second-floor bathroom illuminated. Had Harper been in there the whole time? Did she have the chance to save her that night?

The sky turned the darkest shade of gray it possibly could. She sprinted toward the front door, all the while the rain pelted and soaked her to her bones. Unbeknownst to her, Penny stepped over another gum wrapper.

She knocked on the door and waited for Peter to answer. Several seconds passed, but she didn't hear anyone inside.

"Peter! Open up!" She pounded against the door again.

Tears streamed down her cheeks and mixed with the rain on her face. Melting together, forging rivers of despair down to her chin.

Finally, Peter opened the door a sliver, and his eyes bulged out of his head. "Penny! What are you doing here?"

The distinct scent of bleach emptied from the house and stung Penny's nostrils. Peter's eye twitched. He looked past Penny as though to see who else may be on the porch steps.

"Let me in," Penny said. "We need to talk."

Peter craned his neck behind him. "Now's not a good time."

"Let me in, Peter! Come on; it's storming out here," Penny pleaded.

"I'm sorry. Not today." Peter moved to close the door, but Penny put her foot in between the door and its frame. Peter stared at her in disbelief. "What's gotten into you, Penelope?"

"It's about Jayson," she replied.

Peter nodded as a shadow crossed his face. His entire demeanor changed; he relaxed. Peter opened the door and beckoned her inside. Then, he closed the door behind her and not only locked it with the deadbolt but pulled the golden chain across it, too. Penny looked around the house she'd been in hundreds of times. Nothing looked different and yet, something felt off. The wooden floors sparkled and Penny noticed a mop, bucket, and empty bottles of Pine-sol and bleach lay near the kitchen.

"So, what about Jayson?" Peter questioned.

Penny ambled toward the red suede couch and plopped down. She pulled her knees to her chest and rubbed her eyes, smearing yesterday's mascara. Penny opened her mouth and closed it. Her jittery legs convulsed against her body no matter how tightly she hugged them.

Peter stood by the front door with his arms crossed and tapped his foot. "Go on," he quipped.

Penny cleared her throat. "Well, it's just that he told me he saw something last week."

Peter narrowed his eyes. "You visited him in Arbordale." It wasn't a question, more of a statement.

"Yes," Penny confirmed, licking her lips.

"And?"

Memories of Peter throughout her life flashed before her eyes. His visit to her class where he marveled and explained the art of journalism and how one article could change a person's life. The day he offered her a position at the *Chronicle*. The meeting where he promoted her to Senior Reporter. All the visits to her house to check up on her mother. The Christmas cards. The birthday cards. The lunches on Main Street. The simple smiles in the morning. They all added up to an image in her mind, an image that prevented her from believing he could lay a finger on poor Harper. And yet, the tiniest atom of doubt lingered in her mind. Besides losing his daughter and suffering a divorce, she really didn't know that much about the man outside of work. They mostly talked about her, her mother, and her career. He never opened up about his past. Could he be hiding something?

"He said he saw you take Harper last weekend." Penny's heart sank. She'd finally said it out loud. She tasted the bile rising in her throat.

Peter nodded and smiled. "He said that, huh? What was his excuse for having Harper's sneakers, then?"

Penny sighed, pulled herself up from the couch, and paced the living room. She ran her fingers through her hair and twisted her tangles up into a messy bun. "He said you put them in there. To frame him."

Peter burst into hearty laughter and doubled over. "He actually said that? Oh, Penny! That's too much."

Penny turned around to stare at her boss. Something in his eyes chilled her to her bones.

"You don't honestly believe him, do you?" Peter asked with one last chuckle.

She bit the inside of her cheek. "I'm not sure what to believe," she admitted.

Peter's smile vanished. "Penny—"

"Listen," Penny said, interrupting him. "I don't want to be in the middle of this. But something inside me needs answers. You taught me that, remember? Always trust your gut."

"I remember well," he spat. "I was there all throughout your life. I was there for you when your father died. When you and Jayson broke up. When your mother fell sick. Or did you forget about that?"

Penny's jaw dropped, she'd never seen or heard this side of Peter. "Of course, I remember! You're like a father to me!"

"Then why are you here, Penelope? Do you truly believe I could hurt a little girl?"

Penny walked all around the living room and then peered outside the front window. Rain poured down the windows and blurred the view of the yard. A shiver ran down her spine, and she turned around. "Where were you last Sunday?"

Peter rolled his eyes. "I was here."

"Alone?"

"Yes, alone," Peter sneered.

"Can anyone corroborate that?" Penny cracked each of her knuckles.

Peter shook his head. "You're spending too much time investigating. I think it's all getting to you. And I think you need to leave."

"You're not making it easy for me to believe you right now," Penny said, exasperated.

Peter strode toward Penny. She jumped and felt the wall against her back. Peter smiled faintly and reached for her hands. She accepted his touch, despite the palms of her hands sweating profusely.

He pulled her toward the couch, and they sat down, side by side. Peter looked directly into her eyes. "Listen, Penelope. I know about you and Jayson, okay? I know everything."

Penny opened her mouth but closed it.

"His wife was on to him. He was cracking. I could see it. I know you could see it, too. His entire world was about to come crashing down."

"What does that have to do with anything?" Penny's cheeks reddened, and she looked away.

"Don't you see, sweetheart? He wanted to draw attention away from his affair. He needed his wife and the entire town to look away. To ignore him and his indiscretions."

Penny rocked back and forth on the couch, contemplating Peter's explanation. It wasn't *that* extraordinary or unbelievable. Jayson *had* been acting strangely all week. Could it be because he actually took Harper and then wanted to manipulate her to believe him instead of Peter?

"I don't know who to believe," she said and stared at the floor.

"Believe me, Penny. You know me. I've always been there for you. I wouldn't hurt anyone."

Penny looked up into Peter's eyes. He looked so genuine. All hostility toward her disappeared. He was Peter, *her* Peter. He couldn't have done it. He just couldn't have. She couldn't imagine Jayson necessarily taking Harper either, but between the two, he was the more probable.

"You believe me, right?" Peter asked.

Penny smiled and took a deep breath. "Yes, I do."

Peter exhaled and leaned back on the couch. "Phew. That's great. Let's get dinner this week and catch up on everything, okay? And, I'm thrilled to read your story about Harper's vigil."

"You know about that story?" Penny blushed. Clearly, she wasn't as stealthy as she thought.

"I know everything, little Penny," he said with a smirk.

Penny stood and smoothed her jeans. She could physically feel her anxiety sliding off her shoulders. She couldn't believe she'd thought Peter could be capable of something like that. It was unthinkable!

She stalked toward the door with her keys in hand. "Well,

I should probably head home. I can finish up my story there. I'll see you at layout tomorrow?"

"Sounds good. And think about where you want to go to dinner this week, okay? Or, we could always do lunch at the Crimson Café."

"Sounds good! I'll see you tomorrow." Penny turned around to see Peter clutching his arm, as though he were wounded. A speckle of blood seeped through his shirt. She shrugged it off, though, and opened the front door.

A gust of wind swirled around the door frame. Dozens of crunchy leaves blew inside. Penny chuckled and looked down at the foliage covering her feet. However, the longer she looked at the crunchy stalks from outside, she realized that wasn't all that blew into the house. Penny bent down and picked up a Bubblicious gum wrapper. She twirled it in her fingers, her stomach sinking. She turned around and opened her mouth to ask Peter about the wrapper.

He was already standing there, though, a glint of evil flickering in his eyes. Penny's eyes expanded above her hollow cheeks. She opened her mouth to scream, but Peter took the hammer in his hand and slammed it down onto Penny's skull. She dropped to the floor as blood oozed from her wound and pooled around her.

Peter bent down beside the woman he'd watched grow up and pushed his fingers against the carotid artery in her neck.

She had no pulse.

CHAPTER TWENTY-ONE

SUNDAY, OCTOBER 13, 2019

S omething happens when time no longer matters. When time no longer measures and dictates your life, that's when you are truly free. You'll never grow old. You'll never miss a moment. You'll never live in the past because the past doesn't exist. The future doesn't exist, either. You're just there. You exist, and yet you don't. Nothing else matters anymore.

I'm no longer in pain, and I have no more sadness. It's faded away. Now, I'm just me. I'll never see my family again, but I'm not lonely. Not anymore.

Penny is here with me. And, I've finally met Heather. They're both so nice. There are lots of other little girls with us, too. It's like I have a whole new family. We keep each other company. We're never lonely.

Heather told me not to hate her daddy for what he did to me. She said he was so sad after she was hit by a car, that he wanted a new daughter to love. But he wasn't a bad man. Just a sad man. The other little girls told me not to be sad. That nothing else could hurt us now. The little girls told me almost no one survives Peter. The only one to get away was little Stacy. She got lucky. But we were lucky to have each other now.

When I saw Penny, she hugged me and held me in her arms. She told me how sorry she was that she couldn't save me. I told her it was okay, that no one could have saved me. She told me how much my mommy and daddy loved me. And, knowing that? Knowing that is enough for me.

For so many hours, I was the little lost girl. But now, I've been found, and I'm not alone. We're all here. Every single one of us. It's safe here. We're happy. Things will never be the same, but that's Crimson Falls for you. The place'll chew you up and spit you back out. You can't leave, and you'll never survive it. It's a cursed town, but it's home.

THE CRIMSON FALLS NOVELLA SERIES

Join the Crimson Falls Reader Group on Facebook for more behind the scenes details, exclusive information, and a community to discuss all the novellas in: https://www.facebook.com/groups/CrimsonFallsReaderGroup/

YOUR FREE BOOK

Download *The Man Behind the Flames* today for FREE!

Lucas Finch is a handsome, successful man with a secret. By day he manages clients' finances and by night he fantasizes about killing women. With a passionate fire burning inside his soul, almost nothing can stop him.

When Lucas plans to commit his first murder, something goes terribly wrong. Lucas must use his wit and intellect to keep the darkness within himself, hidden from view before his entire life is set ablaze.

Thrilling and chilling, *The Man Behind the Flames* provides a unique perspective to the charmingly evil man readers meet in *When Houses Burn*. This prequel will set fire to everything you've imagined about life with a psychopath.

ALSO BY LAURÈN LEE

Coming Home (Detective Dahlia Book 1)

Chasing Death (Detective Dahlia Book 2)

Capturing Evil (Detective Dahlia Book 3)

Chancing Fate (Detective Dahlia Book 4)

Challenging Time (Detective Dahlia Book 5)

When Houses Burn

Cranberry Lane

Running in Circles

We'll Begin Again

The Scanner

Little Girl Lost

Charlotte's Pact (Demons in New York Book 1)

Liam Rising (Demons in New York Book 2)

Adriel's Reckoning (Demons in New York Book 3)

ACKNOWLEDGMENTS

Thank you, reader, for taking the time to read *Little Girl Lost*!

I'd like to thank my beta readers, Emerald, Sal, Greta, and Rachel. Couldn't have done it without you :)

Thank you, Amabel, for editing my book. Loved working with you!

Thank you again, Emerald, for all of your hard work you put into managing this project. You're a rockstar and an angel xoxo.

And, last but not least, thank you to the whole Crimson Falls crew. This was such a fun project, I loved working with everyone!

.

ABOUT THE AUTHOR

Laurèn Lee was born and raised in Buffalo, New York, but currently resides in Tampa Bay, Florida. She loves hockey, football, chicken wings and spending time with her husband, son, family, and friends.

Reading and writing are her life's passions and becoming a full-time author is her ultimate dream. As a child, Laurèn fell in love with the Harry Potter series, and as an adult, she loves psychological thrillers and mysteries with a twist.

Make sure to sign up for her Email Newsletter to be the first to know about new releases, sales, and giveaways!

For more information, visit LaurenLeeAuthor.com

Made in the USA
Columbia, SC
22 May 2022

60779698R00086